SPEEDBUMPS IN THE MIDDLE OF THE SEA

FIREBALL

ARPress

ARPress
45 Dan Road Suite 36
Canton MA 02021

Hotline: 1(800) 220-7660
Fax: 1(855) 752-6001

Ordering Information:
Quantity sales. Special discounts are available on quantity purchases by corporations, associations, and others. For details, contact the publisher at the address above.

Printed in the United States of America.

ISBN-13:   Paperback   979-8-89389-827-9
                eBook   979-8-89389-829-3
                Hardback   979-8-89389-828-6

Library of Congress Control Number: 2024923376

CONTENTS

As of the time of this writing, the characters identified as G and K have since passed away.

INTRODUCTION

*O*h no, not ANOTHER "This is my life" type of book! But, as you can see from the title, this book promises to raise a few giggles, guffaws and in general, to be hilarious. I tested various stories incorporated herein amongst my friends and co-workers, so I can gauge the reaction of most readers. Yes, there will be groans, and yes there will be a few raised eyebrows and eyes rolled up, but there will also be a generous supply of riproarious laughter.

I have thoroughly enjoyed the works of authors such as the late Erma Bombeck and Jean Kerr. These were ordinary folks relating their daily experiences in a humorous way to the public. I sincerely believe that my life experiences are just as hilarious, and the constant encouragement from my friends and co-workers to publish my life experiences has finally resulted in this. So sit back and relax. Be prepared to release your pent-up frustrations and tensions through the medium of laughter.

Originally, this book was to be called "From Mosquito Net to Internet," but there is no story linking the two together. Also, the title does not convey the atmosphere of humour and hilarity. With my Victoria experience, the current title was a natural. The reader is bound to be curious to know HOW can there be "Speedbumps in the middle of the sea"? By picking up this book, it will lead him / her into a humorous adventure.

The stories in this book are all true, but not necessary told in a chronological sequence. My sincere thanks to all my friends and co-workers who made the stories in this book possible.

FINGER DIPPIN' GOOD

In the office where I used to work back home, it was the tradition for the Company to treat the staff to a year-end party at a local five-star hotel, a sister company of our company. But this year, they decided to do things a little differently. Instead, we were to be treated to an outdoor barbecue and we were allowed to bring our families along. Since this was the first time the company had done anything like this, there were bound to be foul-ups. There were not enough barbecue grills or people to barbecue the meat so the going was really slow. We, the more affluent members of society decided to let the less affluent amongst us go first in the queue so that they may eat first. To make things worse, it started to rain heavily, so the food was spoiled. Good thing there was a shelter nearby, so we all went there.

The Company had invited a local famous doctor to give us all a little talk, so he told us of his experiences in the olden days, when he used to teach medicine. In this class, there were about 100 students. The doctor mentioned to the class that the difference between a good doctor and an average doctor was that a good doctor paid attention to details. In those days, the only way to test for diabetes was to taste the person's urine. So he wanted all the class to dip their fingers in the flask of urine and lick, like he had just demonstrated. So the flask went round from student to student, each student dutifully dipping their fingers in the flask and licking, and remarking: "YUCK". Finally, the flask was returned to the doctor who commented to the class: "If you had been good doctors, you would have observed that I dipped this finger in the flask but put this finger in my mouth."

A group of us, S, G, K and myself, were always together, so we decided that we were hungry and bored. We decided not to eat a full meal, as this would spoil our appetites for the evening with our families, but instead to go for coffee and cakes. We now had to decide where, and we ended up at the five star hotel where the Company would have treated us normally. As we entered, we saw a cake trolley, so we decided to seat in a booth at the back. When the waiter came for the order, we asked him what types of cakes he had. Instead of bringing the trolley to us, he would go to the trolley and return to us with a description of the merchandise! So we decided to make things easy for this dumb waiter and ourselves so in desperation we asked him to bring anything that he had, all the same for all of us. He only had three slices maximum of any one kind of cake, so we asked him to bring that, and I would choose something else. So I asked: "Do you have X?"

"No."

"Do you have Y?"

"No."

"Do you have Z?"

"No."

In frustration, I asked: "Do you have fruit salad?" knowing that in a tropical country, this was a common item. Finally he said, "Yes" so I asked him to bring it. Meanwhile, the coffee and cakes arrived and S who used to put in a lot of overtime in the computer section, mentioned that due to the nature of his job, he regretted that he could not be more regular in attendance to the mosque, and wished he could be more so. I therefore offered him some advice. This was in the days when I was not seriously religious. There was pin-drop silence as my friends wanted to hear WHAT advice I would give. My advice to him was simple. He should eat papaya, a natural laxative. K & G started laughing, and after a while S caught on to the joke. He himself admitted that he was a tube light.

Finally my fruit salad arrived. Being a five star hotel, the fruit salad arrived in a fancy container. They had scooped the fruit out of a pineapple, leaving a hollow shell and in this they had filled the fruit salad. It consisted of pineapple, mango, strawberries, papaya, passion fruit, watermelon and banana. The salad was stacked high so I asked my friends if they would like to share it with me and they politely declined as they had already eaten their cakes, I mentioned to S that it had papaya to keep him regular and he declined my offer, so I finished the salad myself. In the pineapple shell, all the fruit juices had accumulated, so I told my friends: "Since you did not help me finish the fruit salad, I'll pass this around. Everybody dip their fingers and lick!"

G looks at me and says: "Don't be disgusting!"

Me: "But it's only fruit juice!"

G: "I don't want to know!"

So I drank the whole thing myself. I could not help remarking: "You know something, that pineapple had diabetes!"

MY OLD HOMETOWN, ATLANTA

In Atlanta, the winters are usually mild, whilst the summers can be severe. People have been known to die of heat waves every summer. I used to work for an electronics retailer, and managed one of their stores in the country. In those days, East Indian people were a rarity and the local white people were, at best bigoted. The Company had a tradition of giving away free beach balls with their name on it for the summer. We normally received our shipment two weeks before they were to be given away in May. So I made a sign on our signboard, with beach balls stuck all over it, that read: DO YOU HAVE BALLS FOR THE SUMMER? Many people would comment on the sign and I would innocently hand out beach balls to the customer. When they saw me and heard my accent, they figured that since I was a "foreigner" I would not realize the implications of the sign. One country farmer came into the store and his face was all red. He shouted angrily: **"I WANT TO SEE THE MANAGER!"**

Me: "That's me."

He looks at me, and all colour drains from his face and he says "Oh." He then purchased something small as an excuse and left the store. The next day, our District Manager came to see me and he was laughing as he entered the store. I knew why he came to see me, but as I was busy with a customer, we didn't get to talk for a few minutes. When we were finally alone, we had a good laugh, but he made me remove the sign after one week because he was getting too many complaints.

Before I got my store in Atlanta, I worked for a manager at a store downtown, and it was a hang out for drunks and hookers. NONE of our customers was a business executive, though skyscrapers were plenty just a few yards away. We had a constant problem with burglaries. The drunks would smash the glass windows and steal all the display merchandise. They could not get into the main part of the store as it had heavy barricades. So I suggested a plan to my manager and he agreed. What I suggested to him was that instead of displaying good merchandise, we should display empty boxes that showed pictures of the merchandise (with the Styrofoam packing and manual removed); defective merchandise that had been written off but looked good on the outside, and discontinued merchandise whose retail sales value had devalued to maybe 5% of the original price. We were now ready for the thieves. Sure enough, they did hit, but it was for the last time, as they must have realized that we had wised up. One fool came to us the NEXT day with merchandise that we recognized as written off, and wanted it repaired free under warranty! We asked him for the receipt, and since he could not produce one, he was stuck with the defective merchandise. When we told this to our District Manager and the Insurance Adjuster, we had a good laugh. The thieves must have told other thieves about their lousy pickings, as we never had another break-in.

For the next couple of articles some knowledge of the Bible is necessary. For those whose Biblical knowledge is weak, here are the relevant verses. St. Paul, on the road to Damascus, had a dream. In that dream it was mentioned to him:"In hoc signo vinces" which is Latin for:" Under this sign you will conquer."

When Jesus Christ (PBUH) was in the process of selecting his helpers (disciples) lots of people came to him but he selected only a handful. His famous words were:" Many are called but few are chosen."

My friend's mother had a whole lot of credit cards. One of the Credit Card companies was running a contest for a slogan and had sent all cardholders an entry form with the bill. Before my friend or the mother had a chance to write anything, I had already written and sealed the form. My entry was: "In hoc up to my neck". In American slang, hoc means debt. Needless to say my entry did not win the contest, but can you imagine the looks of the people who had to read the entry and the faces of the judges?

As I mentioned above, the winters in Atlanta are usually mild. If it snows more than half an inch, the entire city is closed, as they do not have a way of dealing with that quantity of snow. This one year, my friend and

I were visiting a friend and we had stayed over for supper. All of a sudden the lights went out. Atlanta had just been hit by the worst ice storm in 25 years. We managed with candles, finished the meal and had to stay over. The phones were down so we could not call the mother to let her know about us. We heard on a transistor radio next day that the supermarkets were giving away free frozen food instead of throwing it out. We called the mother the next day to explain, I went over to the nearest supermarket somehow and headed straight for the frozen section. Many of the packets there had already gone soft from thawing but here and there one could still find packets that had not yet thawed. The moral of the story? MANY ARE COLD BUT A FEW ARE FROZEN.

I had a chance to use the above punch line almost 12 years later in Switzerland. I was sent to Zurich by the Company I worked for, for further training. The classroom was small and not well ventilated. As a result, it would become very stuffy very quickly, so every hour, during our breaks, I would open the windows to let the fresh air in. Since the heat was on, the place would soon become warm again. This went on for a few weeks, when one student complained. The instructor then requested me not to open the windows, so I asked for a show of hands. When I asked how many people were freezing, a couple of hands went up, but when I asked how many were merely cold, many hands went up. So I told the instructor that there was a moral to this i.e., MANY ARE COLD BUT FEW ARE FROZEN.

SIGNS OF THE TIMES

Over the years I have seen many signboards and below are some of the funny ones I remember:

Sign outside a tailor's: AS YOU RIP, SO SHALL WE SEW.

Sign outside a church: CH – CH. WHAT'S MISSING? UR

Sign outside a laundry: SPECIAL OF THE WEEK: SHIRTS 99c. Some joker had removed the R

Sign outside a repair shop: CLOCK WON'T TICK? TOCK TO US.

Sign on a dairy farm delivery truck: WE OWE OUR SUCCES TO UDDERS. Underneath someone had spray-painted: AND THAT'S NO BULL.

Sign outside a local business: WE CAN'T SPELL S CCESS WITHOUT U

Sign outside a home: THE DOG'S OK. BEWARE OF THE WIFE

INTELLECTUALLY CHALLENGED WAITERS

My uncle swears that the following is a true story. He and his cousin were students at Cambridge University in England, during the sixties. During the break between classes, both my uncles would go to the café across the campus. My uncle would always order coffee, whilst the cousin would always order tea. Usually, they would be attended by another student, also an East Indian. The waiter must have served them dozens of times, so one would expect that by now he would remember their likes and dislikes. But no, the waiter would always ask what they would like to order. So one day, they decided to play a prank on the waiter. When they were asked by the now familiar waiter what they would like to order, they placed their usual order. When the waiter arrived with the order, he asked, "Who's having coffee?" and my uncle indicated that he was. The waiter then asked, "Who's having tea?" and the same uncle said he was. So the waiter placed the coffee AND the tea with him and left.

This happened to me and my friends at a beach resort during New Year's Eve celebrations.

The hotel in question is in Mombasa, on the Equator. The weather there can be stifling hot, even at night. So it was only natural that I had finished my soda with the meal, and I wished to order some more. Our waiter was a little slow intellectually, to say the least. Instead of taking orders for several people at a time and arriving with a tray full, he would take each order individually to the bar and return with ONE item. At a time like New Year's Eve, obviously the place was overcrowded. I had ordered my soda at around 11:30, but in vain. I had not received my order by 11:45, or by 11:55PM. The minutes to midnight ticked away, and in desperation I had to toast the New Year with melted ice. My drink arrived 15 minutes past midnight, with the bill. I really let the waiter have it. "I ordered my soda LAST year. You are bringing it THIS year. It's only fair that I should pay you NEXT year!"

He was livid and he called the manager, who knew my friends and me. We laughed and assured the waiter that it would be paid.

DISKETTE HUMOUR

One of the companies I worked for, was really tight fisted, to say the least. To give you an example, if we wanted a pencil, we had to submit the stub of the old pencil first. Similarly, if we wanted a ball- point pen, we had to submit the old one that quit working. One bright day, the Chairman decided that every Department Executive deserves a personal computer, so my department head received a PC but no printer. What good is that? That's like ordering sports shoes but no laces. I learnt how to use it, and to print the document, I had to wander from department to department to find an available printer and print the documents. We complained to the Financial Controller, who said that we should request for it in the upcoming budget, which we duly did. The printer arrived, but the FC took it for his own department and told us to request one for the following year's budget. So we went another year without a printer. Meanwhile, I continued to wander from place to place in search of a printer for the documents. Needless to say, in the process my diskette must have picked up a virus, which was transferred to a PC in the FC's department. When he found out that I had last used the PC, he called me in his office and I was blunt: "If we had our own printer, I would not have to wander from place to place, and I would not have picked up the virus!" He could not argue with that!

A virus scan revealed that the diskette was only 78% usable, so I had to update the back-up diskette and use that. Now, in order to get a replacement diskette, I had to submit a WHOLE BOX of defective diskettes! When would I accumulate an entire box of defective diskettes? So I was stuck with the defective one. No point throwing it away, as there was strict accounting for EVERY item supplied. So

I reformatted the diskette and used it to write jokes and funny anecdotes on it. An example of such humor appears at the end of this article. I now had a diskette full of humour. I would carry that with me whenever I traveled from department to department, and whenever I found a secretary's desk unoccupied, I would quietly and innocently slip that diskette in her IN tray. There were no markings or labels on the diskette. When she returned to her desk and found the diskette, she would obviously check with her boss (the Department Executive) whether he / she had placed it there. When her boss denied knowledge, she would be honour bound to return it to the rightful owner. She would insert the diskette and start reading. The index was a garble of letters that only I could decipher, so she would be forced to open one of the files. She would read and start laughing. No need to ask where the diskette came from! Inevitably, I would end up with the diskette and I would be on my way for the next "victim". If anyone called, my secretary would inform the caller that I was in this department or that. I always had an alibi.

Here are some examples of the humour:

The carnal desires of a camel
Are more than anyone thinks.
This wild and hoary mammal
Has desires on the hole of the Sphinx.
But at times his object of desire
Is covered with the sands of the Nile
Which explains the camel's expression
And the Sphinx's inscrutable smile!

There was a woman of Penzance,
Who taught young men to dance.
But a student named Wong,
Got a few steps wrong.
Do you know of an abortionist, by chance?

Tell me she can keep a straight face after reading this!

WINDOWS 95

I worked for an electronics retailer in Victoria, BC. At this time, there were rumours that our chain of stores would receive advance copies of Windows 95, which of course, was not true. Nevertheless, we got a lot of inquiries. I got tired of sounding like a broken record, telling every customer the same thing. So I decided to have a little fun. A pre-teenager came to me asking me if we had Windows 95. I answered," No, but we do have Air Conditioning 78".

When he asked where I kept it, I pointed to the ceiling. He turns around to complain to his mother, who overheard everything, for she was smiling.

"He's only having a little fun, Dear" was her consoling remark to her son.

SPEEDBUMPS IN THE MIDDLE OF THE SEA

When I first arrived in Victoria, I had no place to stay, so I stayed at a hostel. The hostel had dormitories, with eight bunk beds per room, so I had to move out of there fast. I searched the local papers for a place to stay, and I found a house that was being converted into a rooming house. I was the first customer, so I picked a good room for myself and moved in. In the course of time, eleven people were living in a house made for a family of four. This was unhygienic and unacceptable. In the same place was a girl S who also wanted to move out pronto. We found a decent one-bedroom apartment, and we moved out of the overcrowded house in due course. S referred to it as The Hilton Hell Hole. One day, we were reminiscing. She said:" I wouldn't move back there for all the money in China."

Without missing a beat, I responded: "But there is no money in China".

She replied: "For all the tea, then."

It must have taken a full three minutes for the penny to drop, for she came running to me, screaming: "Of course there's money in China!"

I told her: "It took you this long to figure out? Good thing you are not the President of any corporation. By now, your enemies would have walked all over you."

She saw the logic of that! She was very easy to deceive. Many times during our conversations, I would throw out something at her. For example, at one time she was telling me of her life in Red Deer. So I asked: "How far is that from Blue Nose?"

My question took her by surprise. She spent the next few minutes trying to remember, before she piped up: "There is no such place as Blue Nose in Canada."

"OK. I was only asking."

One day I decided to visit Vancouver, for the first time in my life. I asked her: "So what time is it over there?"

It took her a full three minutes to respond: "The same as here!"

My trip TO Vancouver on the ferry was smooth, but the return trip was choppy. I mentioned this to her. "It must be all the new speed bumps they put in there."

She agreed with me. Only later, after I had taken my shower, did she exclaim," How can there be speed bumps in the middle of the sea?"

"You tell me, you agreed with me. I come from a third world country, what do we folks know of modern technology?" (according to her, anyone who was non-white was a "dumb foreigner", so I played that card to the fullest).

MOTHER'S LOGIC

When I was a kid, I was extremely mischievous. My mother would visit her sister at the local elementary school, where she was the Head Mistress. The school had a newly built swimming pool, so I would take a dip in it while my mother and her sister gossiped. One day, I must have been in the pool hardly a few minutes, before it started to rain. So my mother starts shouting at me: "Come on, we are going."

"But we just got here."

"Can't you see it's raining?"

"So?"

"YOU'LL GET WET."

After thirty years, I'm still trying to figure out the logic of this.

BETWEEN A ROCK AND A HARD PLACE

My parents decided to visit Hong Kong without me, so I had the entire house to myself. I was in my teens, so my grandmother and my uncles and aunts would periodically pop in to see how I was doing. I would call a few friends over, and we would listen to the latest tunes on my stereo. This got boring too soon, so I decided that we could also do a little sightseeing. Before my father left, he told me that a friend of his had given us open invitation to visit his game lodge and stay for free any time. Well, I told my friends about it, so we decided to take him up on his offer. It was our school break season, so we had all the time in the world. My friends took permission from their parents, and the three of us headed out, with cameras and my father's Mercedes Benz. We stayed at the lodge a few days. We saw every animal except lions. We were told that there were some lions at a certain location, so we headed out. As we were driving along, the car got stuck in a bog and refused to move. We had no choice but to make tracks to the lodge and get help. So we started walking with the stereo going full blast to scare the animals. We finally arrived at our destination. When we told the staff what happened, we were given a severe scolding. Didn't we know it was unsafe? They took us in their SUV to the spot we indicated. The ranger told us to look in the bushes on the left and on the right of us. You know of the expression "Between a rock and a hard place"? We saw lions on one side, cheetahs on the other. We passed between them to get to the lodge. Apparently, the lions were waiting for the cheetahs to attack, and the cheetahs were waiting for the lions to attack, and we escaped unhurt. It is only by the Grace of Almighty God that we are still alive to tell the tale.

LUNCH CLUB

$\mathcal{B}$ack home, we get paid once a month. Therefore, when we receive our salaries, it is an occasion for celebration. We would be paid in two installments: Fifteen percent of our salary would be in cash, and the balance would be deposited to our account. This way, we could buy groceries, etc before we got around to withdraw money from the bank. There was no such thing as Interac in those days. Since we had brown-bagged our lunches for most of the month, a group of us decided that once a month we could afford to have a decent lunch. We used to get 75 minutes for lunch, so we would go to a decent restaurant, and split the bill. We would budget $15 per person. We explored all types of cuisines. One day I took the group to a French restaurant, with the intention of sampling escargot or frogs' legs. As luck would have it, the restaurant was out of both items. One girl overheard my request, and when we returned to the office, she asked me if I was serious about frog's legs. I told her I was, so she told me that she could order frozen frogs legs from her friend in Zaire. When she would receive them, she would call me. I thought she was merely pulling my leg, so I consented. A couple of months later, she called me to her office to tell me the frogs' legs had arrived. I still did not believe her, but she asked me to ask our group when would be a convenient date for dinner instead of lunch. I asked all the members of the group and reported this to M, who then asked me how her chef should prepare the item. I asked what the choices were. "Either the traditional French style, or as a curry".

I opted for curry, since if anything stuck out as different, our friends would be loath to try anything new. The whole purpose was to ensure that they all tasted the new food item. I was under oath not to mention this to anyone, and I readily obliged. I informed the members of the date and place of the dinner.

On the date of the dinner, when we sat at the table, the chef brought out the frogs' legs and chapattis (East Indian flat bread). This was the appetizer. Obviously people asked what it was, and they were told "Chicken curry." Everyone had thoroughly enjoyed it. Some of us had two or even more helpings. When the main dish arrived, that too was chicken. So everyone asked what it was we just ate. That's when I let the cat out of the bag. "Oooo, gross" were some of the kindest remarks I heard. I told them it was already too late to complain, since they had already eaten and enjoyed the delicacy. The rest of the dinner went without a hitch.

BURGLARPROOF CAR

*B*ack home, cars are a luxury, and status cars even more so. My friend's friend was a mechanic, and he had wired up his covetous car in a way to fool the burglars. I do not remember the exact details, but suffice it to say that none of the instruments did what they were originally designed to do. The horn might be the ignition; the wiper switch may turn on the radio, etc. He would deliberately leave the car unlocked, daring any thief to steal it. Needless to say, no one did. No one but he knew the exact function of the various devices and switches on his car.

NO CONNECTION

$\mathcal{O}$ne of the girls in the Accounts Department back home, decided to leave her job and start her own business. She was telling me and another girl on our lunch club about it. When I asked what she would be selling, she replied:" Furniture and electronics".

I naturally assumed that this would be office furniture and office electronic equipment, such as ABC Office Supplies, and asked her this in confirmation.

She said, "No. It will be mattresses and radios."

I flipped. "But what's the connection?"

"These days you don't need a connection!"

So I continued: "Well, in that case, next time you need your hair done, let me know. I'll talk to my mechanic. He can use the spark plugs as hair rollers; the exhaust can be the hair dryer, I'm sure he can do a good job. You don't need a connection right?"

"Talk sense!"

"I'm talking the same sense as you!"

Her friend came to her defense. "What Y is saying is that she will have two lines of business. If one fails, another takes over."

Y piped up: "When someone comes to my store for a radio, doesn't he remember he needs a new mattress?"

I could contain it no longer. "So let's advise Joe to sell mosquito nets from his deli. After all, he will have two lines of business. If the food business dies, the mosquito net business can take over. When someone is enjoying his meal, doesn't he realize he needs a new mosquito net?"

Her friend came to her defense yet again: "We must all support our ex-staff in their business. So why don't you visit her store sometimes?"

"Sure, when my sofa blows its fuse, I'll know where to go."

I visited her store. In a small hole in the wall, she intended to create a department store. In one corner she had sofas, stacked one upon the other, to the ceiling. The sofa column was leaning precariously; it is a miracle that the Leaning Tower of Sofa did not fall on anyone and cause injury. In another corner she had bicycles. In the display case inside, she had, cassettes, batteries, bias binding, hurricane lamps, bath soap and shoelaces. The store could not have been much bigger than a Chinese take out restaurant. When I went home, I composed this article. Be warned, there is NO CONNECTION. So don't try to make sense of it.

JUST ARRIVED from the vineyards of Alaska, with sawdust dressing, and re-introducing for the first time to BC by popular demand: NEW AND IMPROVED BIODEGRADEABLE CHOCOLATE SYMPHONY IN SERGEANT MAJOR.

FEATURES:

Chrome plated, auto focus, daisy wheel, barbecued mosquito net with fluoride @14% interest, compounded semi-epileptically. Guaranteed rustproof, kills 100 cockroaches per minute, fully air-conditioned and IBM compatible. Responds to the name Hong Ding Dwah, potty trained, inoculated against Microsoft and allergic to Oxygen. Your choice of Kosher Diesel in 7.5 fragrant colours OR nonfattening enamel with vitamin enriched retreads to cure constipation. FREE EKG with every major overhaul. Available only at:

No Connection Inc., Marine Drive, Northern Sub- Sahara, only 13 Kgs. Past St. Karl Marx's Temple of the Underground Opium Oasis. Payment in US Orang-Utangs only. Batteries not circumcised. Allow halitosis for delivery. Pat. Pend. Complies with FCC regulations on pre-digested spark plugs.

IF YOU UNDERSTOOD THIS, YOU HAVE A GREAT FUTURE AS A NUCLEAR SNAKE CHARMER.

MESSAGE RECEIVED

I am sure you have heard some people's answering machines that specify: "After you have finished, you may hang up or dial one for more options." I got tired of hearing that line so when I got my answering machine, I recorded on my outgoing message tape: "After you have finished, you may hang up, or dial 911 for more options".

One of my duties back home, was to arrange for medical examinations for customers who purchased life insurance. One day this woman comes storming into my office, practically demanding that I rebook her for urinalysis. I looked through my planner and noted that her appointment was booked two weeks prior.

"Yeah, I know, but my car was burgled"

"My sympathies, ma'am, but what's the connection?"

It appears that the lab had given her an empty jar to take home and return to the lab with the sample of the urine from rising in the morning. She must have misplaced the empty jar, as she could not find it. She washed out an empty perfume bottle and used that instead. Her fancy car was parked in front of a fancy restaurant, on the way to the lab, with all her shopping. The thieves took everything from the inside of the car, including the perfume bottle. The funny part is, can you imagine the thief giving the bottle to his wife / girlfriend and her using it?

WHAT'S IN A NAME?

*I*f anyone has ever traveled on the Toronto Subway, then they will realize what I say is true. I firmly believe that the names of the various stations were inspired after a bout of 'flu. I give below MY version of the names, and the cleaned-up version in (). Read, compare and ponder. Here they are:

High Temperature (High Park); Runny Nose (Runnymeade); Bufferin (Dufferin); Hot Bath (Bathurst); Lozenge (Lawrence); Not so good (Osgood); Some are ill (Summerhill); Chest rub (Chester); Green snot (Greenwood); Nauseum (Museum); Nosebleed (Rosedale); Get well soon (Wilson); Len's down with fever (Lansdowne); Tonsils (York Mills); Blow your nose (Bloor) Did I convince you yet?

BUNGLING BUREAUCRATS

How dumb can bureaucrat staff be? Read on and judge for yourself. I had a bet with my friend back home that I could prove the IQ rating of such staff. I hate to call them civil servants, since in most cases, they are NOT civil. I sent a letter to a friend of mine from one city to another IN THE SAME COUNTRY, about 300 miles away. That's like sending a letter from Edmonton to Calgary. Under the address, I had written VIA HONG KONG. The letter was postmarked Hong Kong when my friend received it. For a long time, he had it framed in his house as evidence.

SWEET SLUMBER

When my friend first came to Canada, he had a hard time finding a job. He must have been jobless for 6 months. He lived in Toronto, while I was in Vancouver. I used to come home from work late, so sometimes I would call him up. He would be in deep sleep, due to time difference. My 10:00 PM would be his 1:00 AM. So I had a little fun with him. Whenever he picked the phone, I would tell him: "You're fired," without identifying myself or saying hello. He would ask: "Why?"

How can you be fired from a job you don't have? This went on for a while. One July evening, I told him to look outside his window, as it was snowing, and he looked! Until he realized that it was the midst of Summer, and I was speaking from the other end of the country!

OPEN TO SERVE YOU

In Victoria, at a certain shopping center, one of the drug stores was being torn down and extended. The builders had torn down everything except one wall which still bore their name and proudly announced "OPEN SEVEN DAYS A WEEK" I took a photo and sent it to the local papers, saying, "Of course they are open, not only seven days a week but also 24 hours a day!" A week later, the article appeared in the papers.

A SPADE BY ANY OTHER NAME

I completed my High School in England. During one of the English classes, the teacher decided to give us as homework the use of common phrases and clichés. We had to demonstrate their meanings by using them in sentences. Now, this is a good exercise for ten year olds, but we were to graduate the following semester. So I decided to have some fun. I wrote down some really funny sentences. The next day, we had to read out loud what we had written. One of the phrases was "to call a spade a spade" and my homework read: "Farmer Brown always called a spade a spade until one day, he tripped over it." The whole class laughed, and we never had such assignments again.

FROM HERE TO WHERE?

*I*n Victoria, at the electronics retailer that I worked for, it was common practice that if one branch did not have the goods that the customer wanted, we would call the other stores. The customer could either go to that branch to pick up his merchandise, or we would ship it to the other store. One day, we received a phone call from one store for some merchandise. This customer lived far away, so we had to ship his goods. Since he was paying for the shipment, we had to find the cheapest courier. So I'm talking to the manager of the other store on the phone: "So how are you sending it?" I had decided to send it via Dan Foss Couriers. I decided to have a little fun with the manager. I replied: "Via Dental Floss."

I made my manager laugh in the process.

DETENTION, ANYONE?

I completed my high school in a boarding school in England. Being a private school, we had kids from all over the world, and some local Anglo Saxons. Bullying and racism was a common problem. We had a special time of the day for everyone to complete their homework (known as Prep), so those who had to be punished would lose their privilege of going to town on Saturday afternoons. Teenagers loved to go to town, go to the movies, dates and frolic. Loss of this one afternoon during the week was a big blow. Now, what to do during the afternoon? The Headmaster and his Deputy tried all types of schemes until they hit on the idea that while they had a captive audience, they might as well impart some useful knowledge to the delinquent student. No one learnt anything constructive by writing 500 times: "I Will Not......." Also, whoever supervised the delinquent also had to sacrifice his Saturday afternoon off, so he also lost in the bargain. The solution was to give the delinquent three days to make a list of 100 words beginning with a certain letter of the alphabet, and give their meanings. The delinquent student had a few sheets of paper handed to him with a certain letter in bold red, and the due date. Most kids played sports and so during the Prep period, they were too busy finishing their homework. When did they have time to compile a list of 100 words and their meanings? Since I did not play sports, I would do all my prep during Sports. So now I had plenty of time on my hands. I would do other people's detention for them for a price. I had with me a crossword dictionary that gave one- word synonyms. I made a list of words from all the common letters (there aren't too many words beginning with X, for example) and kept them under lock and key. Whenever someone wanted a list of words, I would sell it to him for a price. If I was given the normal three days notice, the price was only 25 cents, but if he came at the last minute, as the usually did, it cost them $1.00. My excuse was that I did not have enough time to prepare the list at such short notice. If the delinquent student submitted his list before lunchtime on the due date, he was excused detention and could spend the Saturday afternoon in town. I used to hand these over at the very last minute, all crumpled, to show that I had to rush. Since I was the only kid crazy enough to do this unpleasant task, nobody bullied me, since I was a valuable commodity. Who would do their detention if I was in bed and unable to read or write? Plus I increased my vocabulary in the process.

WHAT'S YOUR FAVOURITE DISH?

*I*n the same boarding school, I overheard some kitchen staff complain to the Headmaster that they would not work on Saturdays or Sundays unless they were paid double for those shifts. So I approached the Headmaster and offered my services. I assured him that my Prep would not suffer; if it did, he was free to curtail my services. While the rest of the kids were doing Prep, I was washing the dishes and setting the tables for breakfast the next morning. I made a lot of money. Soon, the Headmaster decided to punish students by having them help me for free. I'm not complaining, for I had more time to myself since the work was done faster. I used to wash the dishes on all three meals on Sunday, and after the evening meals Monday to Friday. Eight meals per week at $5 per meal, gave me a whopping $40 every week as my "pocket money," or as it is called nowadays, allowance. In those days, money had value. A movie ticket used to be $1.50, the latest LP (no CDs in those days) cost $32.00, and the latest single cost $8.00

I used to wait until these songs went OFF the Top 40, and buy these singles and LPs used for less than one third the price. So every week, I would return to the school with a whole bunch of singles and LPs.

SOLAR POWER

$\mathcal{I}$ finally managed one branch of the electronics store I talked about previously, in Atlanta. In those days, solar cells had just come out and every student wished to experiment with these. My store was two or so blocks away from the technical school, so I had a lot of student customers. Now it was fall season and the demand for solar cells was just too high. Our warehouse could not keep enough in stock. So I asked our District Manager for the phone number of the District Manager in Alaska. He wanted to know why I wished to have that number. I proposed to him that the stores in Alaska probably have a lot of these sitting idle (6 months darkness in Alaska) that I could obtain and sell. I finally managed to contact the Alaska DM and requested him to send all the solar cells he could lay his hands on. He was glad for my call, since for his stores, they were merely dead inventory. I used to receive parcels of from two to up to 20 or more cells. I ended up with over 500 of these. Now I had to sell them fast. I called my customers and let each of them know that I could probably supply him with six or eight cells. When he came into the store, I would have a packet of eight to ten cells of assorted size waiting for him. I would tell him that was the best I could do. Since solar cells were not available anywhere else, he had no choice but to take what I offered him. Similarly, I would call up all my other customers and also the technical school instructors. I would make packages of twenty to thirty for the instructor, with the hope that I may be able to get some more shortly. I would then call him up after two or so days with some more. This way, I could sell off all my supply at almost the full retail price (quantity discounts would start from 12 and over) before the month was over. That month, I had the most profit in that store.

DO YOU RECEIVE?

The store I managed in Atlanta was a small store at a strip plaza. About five blocks away was a mall, and ten minutes away a mega mall. These were my constant competition. When I had cornered the market on solar cells, if any of their customers needed any solar cells, I would inform them I had "a couple" and request them to send their customers to my store. This was also the time for electronic gadgetry such as calculators and watches that took button sized batteries. Once again the warehouse could not keep enough in stock. I used to order the popular sizes by the gross from the warehouse. I was not taking any chances. It so happened that I received a call from one of the mall stores to see if I had a certain size battery. Of course I had, but I told the manager I had a few hanging on the peg. So he sent the customer to my store. It was my habit to point out to all customers some items we had on sale. That month we were featuring outdoor TV antennas on sale. I pointed this out to the customer. He told me he was looking at one of these at the mall store. I persuaded him to buy from me thus:

"Yeah, I've been looking at one of these at the other store."

"Since you are already here, and the merchandise is the same in all our stores, can I fetch you one?"

"No, I owe my loyalty to Ken."

"You mean to tell me you came all this way for a $1.99 battery? Make your trip worthwhile. You can do your other shopping at Ken's store."

He walked away with over $200 worth of merchandise. That is in the '70s, so in today's values, it could easily be $600 or better.

A couple of days later I received a phone call from the DM.

"You have been accused of stealing1"

"I've never stole anything in my life!"

"You stole Ken's customer. How did you do that?"

I explained the transaction. He laughed and told me to keep up the good work. Normally, the mall stores steal our sales, as they have larger inventories, and they are likely to have the expensive equipment in boxes, whereas I would normally only have the display models. It's not every day that a small store like mine can be a thorn in the flesh for a mega store.

A GOOD RUN FOR YOUR MONEY

In my youth, I did not care much for sports. I preferred to get my homework done and out of the way, so I could concentrate on play. Consequently, I was a favourite target for bullies at school. I handled them my way. My father suffered from constipation, so in our house we had a steady supply of laxative chocolates and laxative chewing gum. One of my tricks was to rewrap the laxative gum in the wrapper of ordinary gum. Whenever bullies would threaten to beat me up if I did not hand over money, I would simply empty my pockets. Out would fall the laxative gum, wrapped as ordinary gum. The bullies would quickly grab these and consume them, often in my presence, to spite me. I once tried the gum. I had a slight case of constipation. I read the instructions. You were supposed to chew two sticks of gum until all the flavour was gone. I was a little cautious. I used only ONE stick, and threw it out before the flavour ran out. I soon felt the power of the laxative. The bullies ate these by the handful. Needless to say, I did not see them for the next few days. I also used laxative chocolate in a similar manner. Whenever my mother or sister baked some cookies, I would swipe some while they were still hot, and melt a generous amount of laxative chocolate on top, to serve as coating. I would then include these in my lunch box. I would be careful not to eat these, but at the recess or lunch break, the bullies were welcome to them. The results were just as devastating. Nobody could link the "stomach upset" with me so I was safe.

STARRY, STARRY NIGHT

I used to live on the very top floor of an apartment building. I got to know one widow with a teenage daughter. I would visit them often, sometimes carrying food or goodies. One night the subject of stars in the sky came up, so I asked the daughter if she could identify the stars in the sky. She could not, and as the sky was clear, I proceeded to take her to the window and give her a lesson in astronomy. "See that red one? That's Mars. That haze is the Milky Way. Those three in a row are Toblerone." At this point the mother started laughing.

The daughter still did not catch on, so I continued: "Those four in the corner are Fruit and Nut." That's when she caught on. We had a good laugh.

NOTE: Mars, Milky Way, Toblerone and Fruit and Nut are various names of chocolate bars.

OUT TO LUNCH

The Lunch Club started on a casual basis. A couple of friends and myself decided to live it up at least once a month when we got our salaries. The news of our adventures spread, until people joined or dropped out as time passed. At one time we must have had over 20 staff members sharing the experience. I used to introduce various cuisines to them. We explored French, Japanese, Chinese, Mex-Tex when that opened up, Greek, Thai, Italian and of course the usual Chinese, Indian and British fares. I took them to what I thought was a Spanish restaurant, but when we got there, it had changed management. It had become a Japanese restaurant. We explored the cuisine there. They ate Sushi (Sea weed) for the first time. I also ordered Red Bean ice cream for desert. One girl was brave enough to try it and also ordered the same, but got cold feet and cancelled her order. When my desert came, I passed it around for all to try. Every one loved it so much, that by the time the bowl returned to me, it was empty. I introduced this desert to the mother and daughter who lived in the same building as myself (see Starry, starry night).

WEEKEND GAME

My department had a lot of expatriate staff as Executives, come and go over the years. I took it upon myself to show them the countryside and the wild game at the game parks. We would leave the city on a Saturday afternoon, arrive at our destination before sunset, and find decent lodgings. We would then explore the game parks the next day. We saw all kinds of wild game, from elephants, lions, giraffes, flamingoes, rhinos, deer and antelopes, ostriches, pheasants, monkeys, cheetahs and leopards, and explore the local cuisine. On a long weekend, I would take them to the seaside almost 6 hours away by car. We would stay at some cheap motel, enjoy the beach, the local food, and return for work Monday morning. On the way we would stop by the roadside fruit vendors and purchase fruits and vegetables at throwaway prices. This way, we got a chance to explore a lot of the countryside, including hot springs, mountain resorts, game parks, lakes, seaside, and sampled the local fare and customs along the way.

I used to carry my camera with me, so I have a lot of memories of these trips. I also made extra copies of the photos for the executives' families for their posterity.

CHEQUES AND BALANCES

When I managed the electronics store in Victoria, I had to make the deposit for the day's business. One particular day the business was almost all returns. When I cashed out, I had a grand total of 62 cents to be deposited! Had it not been for a couple of cheques, it would not be worth it to make a deposit for such a small amount. Unfortunately, the deposit had to be made, by company rules. Otherwise I would lose my job.

WIFE A MEETS WIFE B

My wife had newly arrived from Fiji. We were in bed, after intimate moments, she still had her arms around me. At this point I announced: "I can now tell you. I have two wives." In our culture, we are allowed four wives. Nevertheless, you should have seen the expression in her eyes! So I continued: "Before you get all upset, let me explain that one of them is on two legs, the other on four."

Now she starts to think that I am a pervert. Sheepishly, she asked: "So, who's the four-legged one?"

I told her: "My car!"

She smiled and asked me how a car can be like a wife.

I explained: "She needs to be fed and serviced regularly, or else she will make noises; once in a while she needs to be beautified; she gives me the news of the day; sometimes she even sings to me; she goes wherever I go; she will carry my children; and in the winter, she keeps me warm!"

She had a good laugh.

In her language, the word for leg and wheel is the same.

SKIRTING THE ISSUE

*M*y mother swears this story is true. I have absolutely no recollection of the incident. Make of it what you will:

When I was about five years of age, my parents visited the coastal town of Mombasa, with me in tow. These were the days before air conditioning and pre-independence. Apparently, it was so hot, and I could not tolerate it. So I did the next logical thing. I sought shelter under a white woman's skirt!

Not only that, but, so the story goes, I began pinching her buttocks from my refuge. The woman screamed at my parents to get me out of there. My mother was shy and my father would not attempt to go under a strange woman's skirt, so there was an impasse. How they finally managed to get me out is not very clear to me or to my parents, so I will end this story here and leave the rest to your imagination.

RULES OF THE ROAD

I was new to Canada and had to shop around for insurance for my car. Since I had no previous insurance in Canada, I would be quoted the highest rate. The only way to bring down the premium was to enroll in a Driving School and obtain a certificate. I had over twenty years driving experience but all that mattered little. So I enrolled. The subject matter was old hat to me, so I decided to have a little fun in class. The instructor from India asked us what various flashing lights meant:

"What does a flashing green light mean?" Someone answered correctly, "Pedestrian controlled crossing."

"What does a flashing yellow light mean?" Again someone answered correctly, "Proceed with caution."

"What does a flashing red light mean?" This had the class stumped. I put my hand up, so I was called on to answer. "Red light district" was my answer. The instructor fell backwards laughing, but the rest of the class knew not what I said. For your information, in countries where prostitution is legalized, Red Light District is where their activities are confined. Another time the instructor asked the class what was meant by BAC (correct answer: Blood alcohol content). Since the students had not studied the chapter the night before, I had a field day with my crazy answers, among them:

Burger and Chips; Bank AmeriCard (the old name for Visa credit card); Beck and Call. Finally the instructor asked the question to the class once again, saying: "anybody but you!" as he pointed to me. My answers had thoroughly confused everyone. The instructor said to me: "Now see what you've done! You've confused everybody!" I answered: "That's the whole idea. On the road there will be lots to distract the driver. But he or she must remain focused." Finally, someone looked up the answer in the book and read it out loud. Another time, he drew a diagram of a motorist involved in an accident, as reported in that morning's newspaper. He asked the class: "Now what could the driver of Car A have done differently?" Before anyone could answer, I piped up: "Taken the transit!" The whole class laughed on that one!

FOR WHOM THE BELLE TOLLS

My wife went strawberry picking for the first time in her life. She had a lot of bending to do. Consequently, when she came home, her legs and back were aching. I had to massage her for two days before she could even walk. When I told this to a friend of mine, he asked me whether I took advantage of massaging any other part of her body. When I told this to my wife, she told me to tell him that he should put a bell on his privates, so his wife would know when he is horny and ready for her. I told him what my wife had said, and he rolled over in laughter. He assured me he would implement the plan.

THREE-WHEELED BICYCLE

While my wife and myself were on the road, I saw ahead of me a van carrying bicycles on its back rack. It had obviously dismantled one of the bikes, since there were only three wheels showing. I could not resist pulling my wife's leg, so I made a comment: "Look, honey, nowadays bicycles come with three wheels."

She "Where?"

Me: "Look straight ahead."

She saw and made a response: "That's two bicycles."

Me: "Then there should be four wheels. Show me the fourth."

She obviously couldn't, but she did point out that there were two seats.

Me: "That's right, three wheels, two seats, but one bike,"

She was stumped for an answer. She continued to insist there were two bicycles, but could not offer an explanation as to the missing wheel. She must have been pondering over this for the rest of the day, for as we were about to retire for the night, she asked me if I had an explanation. I finally mentioned to her that the bike had probably been dismantled and the missing wheel must be in the van. She laughed hard when she realized how I had tried to hoodwink her. It almost worked!

MY TRIP TO INDIA

When I was a kid, my parents took my sister and me to India. This was over 30 years ago, so the population of India was about half then. We visited Bombay, Calcutta, Delhi, Poona, Agra, Jaipur, Darjeeling, and Lahore and Karachi in Pakistan. When we landed at the airport in Bombay, we had to hold our noses, as the people were sleeping and shitting not far from the runaways. I told my father I wanted to go back home. We had to hold our noses almost everywhere in India. I remember visiting Chopati in Bombay, where they serve all kinds of ice creams. We tasted the best of Kulfis there! Yummy. On the roads we saw hawkers hawking their goods. The flies were everywhere including on the goods, and the people who bought it ate the dirty stuff! YUK! The beggars were there too. If you gave to one, there would be a lineup of thousands. The funny thing is, the beggars had their price! If you gave anything less than a rupee (Equivalent to $5 today!) they would throw it back at your face! In those days 16 Annas made one rupee, and the decimal currency had just been introduced. So we frequently got change in annas and paisas.

Due to foreign exchange controls in Kenya, we had made arrangements to borrow money in India, and we would credit their account in Kenya when we got back. We were told to go to this particular house, where the rich man lived. We went to a neighbourhood that would make the slums of most cities look posh. We had to climb three or four flights of wooden stairs, where the sodden masses lived, slept and shat. We had to side step them to climb the rotting stairs. When we entered this "house," it was nothing more than a single room. In one corner was the kitchen, in another was the excrement, in one corner was a safe simply bulging with its contents. We had asked for an amount that would be equivalent to today's $50,000 and we were handed a thin wad of cash. It made not the slightest difference to the contents of the safe. That's like removing one spoon of water from a bathtub full. As the man gave the money to us, he asked, "Is that all?" Imagine what's in the safe! And this is how he lives?

We visited Calcutta, and went to a suburb called Dum Dum where the movies were made in those days. We saw the shooting of a scene where the actress had to cry. We saw them retake the scene a few times. Every time the actress had to redo her make-up. When we left, we got an advance free copy of the LP (No CDs in those days!) of the movie they were shooting, Phir Wohi Dil Laya Hoon. The song the actress was supposed to be singing as she cried was "Aankhon se jo uteri". Calcutta is the city made famous by personalities such as Mother Teresa, Ravi Shankar, Ustad Ali Akbar Khan, etc.

We visited a few friends in Madras where they ate hot hot hot curry on banana leaves. We had to have a fire brigade as stand by. We also went to Darjeeling. The regular trains would only go so far. The rest of the journey was on trains that had claws instead of wheels. It was so cold, we stayed indoors by the fire for the few days we were there. What a waste! The scenery was awe inspiring, though!

We of course had to see the Taj Mahal in Agra. What a lovely sight and what a sad story. We Fed the squirrels on the grounds with nuts. They would come up to our hands to eat.

We visited a city that is called the Pink City. (Jaipur). My father had a theory as to how it became pink; the people spat everywhere after eating paan, making the city pink.

We could eat delicious thaali food for only ONE rupee per person! But very hot and spicy. We of course drank a lot of laasi as the food and the season demanded it. It also prevented us from getting the runs, or as my smart ass uncle would say, "Get a good run for your money!"

I was very small at the time, so I do not remember much of the details. I do remember visiting all the touristy spots, and all the landmarks, tombs, etc.

QUESTIONS I HAVE ASKED MYSELF

When the tide is out, where does it go? How does it know when to return? Doesn't it ever get lost? ("Gee, Officer, can you direct me to Waikiki Beach? I'm running late"). So what if the Tide is out? Use Cheer!

What happens if the tide fails to show up for two days? Does it come with a note? ("Please excuse the tide's absence. It had the tonsils.") So how can the Tide have tonsils? Same way that the Cheer can have appendix. How can the Cheer have appendix? The same way that the Tide has tonsils!

It is said that if you hold a conch shell to your ear when the tide is out, you hear the roar of the ocean. But nowadays, Mother Nature has gone High Tech. Now what you hear is: "The tide is now out. At the sound, please leave your name and a brief message…."

To shine your shoes you use shoe polish. To shine your furniture, you use furniture polish. To shine your headlights, do you need headlight polish? Or to shine your flashlight, do you need flashlight polish? For a student to shine in school, does he need student polish? There is a song that goes "Shine on Silvery Moon." Does the moon really have a choice? What was the composer thinking? Someone is going to get up in the middle of the night to turn the switch on the moon OFF? To save on the electric bill, right?

Why is fish considered brain food? It was dumb enough to get caught! A group of fish is called a school. So what do they learn in that school? How to avoid getting caught? Or do they learn to indicate before making a left turn, do a shoulder check and if all is clear, turn? I've never seen a fish with indicator lights, so that can't be it. Dolphins are much smarter than ordinary fish, yet a group of dolphins is known as a POD! What kind of a pod? Pea pod? Cocoa pod? A tri pod? Shouldn't a group of dolphins be known as a college of dolphins or even a university of dolphins? Baby dolphin to sardine: "I just graduated from the Royal College of Dolphins!"

There is a place in BC called Salmon Arm. I never knew fish had hands! Is this where fish fingers come from? Why not name the place Cod Legs? ("Gee, Honey, you have cod legs!"). Or even halibut elbows? What about mackerel knees? If you think that is a stupid name for a town, try this: There is a place in Alberta called Medicine Hat! Why not Injection Gloves? Bandage Bra? Capsule Shorts? Who comes up with such funny names of towns?

Strawberry jam tastes like strawberry. Raspberry jam tastes like raspberry. What does traffic jam taste like? Or a paper jam (in the fax machine or photocopier)? Do these jams come in the same kinds of varieties as the other jams found in supermarkets? Can you imagine the following traffic copter report: "There is a traffic jam on Highway 99 at 911 exit. It looks like sugar free right now, but later on it could turn into traffic marmalade."? Can you imagine your fax machine giving you the following options?

Paper jam. Please select one of the following: (1) Regular. (2) Sugar free. (3) Organic (4) Low Calorie (5) I prefer paper marmalade."

Which raises the question: Is the fax machine, in the offices of Life magazine, the fax of Life?

Everybody knows why the chicken crossed the road. But why did the ostrich cross the road? It was the chicken's day off! So what happens if you eat chicken and egg at the same meal? (e.g. kukoo paka containing boiled eggs). Aren't you eating the mother and the child? For a while, the two will "re-unite" in the stomach. Isn't this what Paul Simon means in his song "Mother and Child Re-union."?

Speaking of songs, there is a song by Bread called "IF". One of the lines in that song is "If a face can launch a thousand ships, then where am I to go?" Let's analyze this song. In my limited experience and knowledge, ships are launched by smashing a champagne bottle against the hull. If a FACE were to launch a ship, the woman would have to be suspended upside down by a bungee cord, and swung so that her face smashes against the hull. OUCH! Would she survive the ordeal, let alone agree to 999 more launches?

I don't think so. I do believe the song has been cleaned up. Instead of the word SHIPS, replace it with SHITS. Now the song makes sense. The woman must have been so ugly that whoever saw her, had to dirty their pants. Isn't the song really asking: "Where is the nearest washroom?" Think about it!

If the earth is spherical, how can we speak of the Four Corners of the Earth? Hold an orange in your hand. Where do you see any corners? The shortest distance between two points is also supposed to be a straight line. That may be fine on PAPER, but on planet Earth, since the Earth is spherical, ALL lines connecting two points will also be curved. Try it out on the orange. Mark two points at least 1 cm apart. Now try to connect the two with a ruler. Can't be done, can it? So who says it must be a straight lion? Why not a lesbian rhino or a gay cheetah? What about the greatest distance between two points? Would that be a transvestite crocodile? Or a celibate gorilla? Who comes up with all these theories, anyway?

If Reader's Digest merged with Dairyland, would you get condensed milk? If Laidlow Recycling merged with Forest Lawn Funeral Parlours, would you get recycled death, i.e. reincarnation? Why does the word reincarnation mean rebirth? Let's analyze the word and see. The word can be broken down into its components rein and carnation. If you combine the flower carnation with horse controls (reins), you get….nope, that can't be it. Let's try rein, car and nation. You are in your car with a copy of the Daily Nation and a set of horse controls….no, it can't be that either. The only explanation possible is that Noah Webster was drunk that day. He wanted to take a bath, but the scribbles came out as rebirth. What's your explanation?

If fish is indeed brain food, should we not fry everything we eat in fish oil? Perhaps the most consumed fried food is chips (French fries). If we fry these in fish oil, every time we eat the chips, we improve our memory. Now, memory chips will have another meaning!

I saw a sign in a window that said "News in Brief." Now, we all know what briefs are: men's underwear! Is this where they are printing the news these days? What next? Cartoons in bra? Stock market report in blouse?

Can you imagine the following conversation at a family brunch: "Honey, can you pass me the classified section please?" "Not now dear, I'm still wearing it!"

Have you ever noticed whose portraits appear on the Canadian bills? If we ignore the $5 and $100 bills as being "extreme values" and look at the middle three, what do you see?

$10 Macdonald

$20 (Dairy) Queen

$50 (Burger) King

Doesn't this tell you something? The whole Canadian economy is financed by the Big Three Fast food franchises! There is no portrait of Wendy's, Tim Horton's or even Zeller's. These are the small guys by comparison! What is your explanation?

RELEVANT OLYMPICS

We all know how the Olympics got their start. In the olden days of Greek rule, sports events were held. Those who excelled in the various sports were inducted into the army. Those who could throw the javelin, for example, could also throw the spear. Those who could jump long distances could also jump across a river. So these skills would be useful in the army. But are the sports of today relevant to our daily lives? Outside of the sports arena, what use is spinning on one's toes on ice? or dribbling a monster ball into a hoop? No, the sports of the modern world should be relevant to our daily lives. For example:

You just missed the bus dash. Contestants should be fully dressed, as if going to work. Briefcases and lunch boxes in hand, these contestants should all race for the bus just as it is about to leave its stop. The object is to get one's briefcase and body into the bus before the door closes.

You overslept again marathon. Contestants have only 15 minutes to wake up from sound sleep, and get their morning routines done, grab a bite of breakfast, have a change of clothes and leave the house.

They will be judged on originality of their routines, e.g. eating breakfast on the bus and on their final appearance / grooming.

Your excuses will get you nowhere scramble. Contestants are confronted by an angry boss who demands an explanation as to their tardiness. Contestants will be judged on the originality of their excuses. "So who's late? I'm just leaving after working the night shift!"

Groceries on a limited budget frenzy. Contestants will be given only a limited amount of cash and time to fill up a cart expecting to feed a family. It is expected that contestants from various countries will have different idea as to what constitutes a family (China vs. Spain) and what constitutes as proper diet in their countries (USA vs. Uganda). The idea is to fill the cart without causing undue damage to other contestants.

Let's see you wiggle out of this one hurdle. Contestants are in bed with their favourite person(s), when suddenly there is a knock on the door. They must answer the door with only a towel draped around them. They will be judged by their reactions to the visitor at the door. Since they have no idea who could be at the door, the answers are completely unrehearsed. The possible visitors are:

The real spouse, soon to be ex.

The mother in law

The parole officer

The boss ("So you're sick, eh?")

Workers' Compensation Board Adjustor ("So you're disabled, eh?")

The principal of the school, with one of the kids of the contestant in tow. To make the game interesting, the principal is always the opposite gender to the contestant, and the child the same gender.

Let's see the contestant handle this one, or we see him / her in court!

ACCIDENTAL INVENTIONS

As we all know, many of today's inventions were discovered by accident. For example, adhesive transparent tape started out as being electrical tape. Someone used it on paper, and today it has become a household product. Ray Kroc, of McDonald's fame, visited Hawaii and introduced the Hula Burger, pineapple ring on top of the beef patty. It was a miserable flop. But pineapple pieces cooked with pizza became a hit. Today, many pizza restaurants offer pineapple as a standard topping. Below are some ideas I propose. Some may go the way of the hula burger, and some may become mega successes. Think of the possibilities:

Hybrid Vegetables.
How do you make your kids eat their vegetables? Try these options:

Chocolate covered steamed broccoli. Kids will eat anything covered in chocolate, so why not vegetables? Currently, chocolate ingredients include nuts, fruits, herbs (mint), so why not vegetables?

Bubble gum flavoured peas. Bubble gum comes in all flavours, including sour varieties. So why not peas?

Strawberry flavoured cabbage. Cabbage should be crossbred with strawberry to resemble the cabbage but taste like strawberries. Just be careful what you use the cabbage for, or you may end up with sweet and sauerkraut!

Cinnamon coated onion rings. We eat onion rings, and then we brush our teeth or gargle with mouthwash to get rid of the smell. So why not coat the onion rings with cinnamon? This will leave fresh smell in your mouth after each bite, saving you the trouble of brushing or gargling. Similarly, mint flavoured garlic, Listerine flavoured smelly cheeses (like Gorgonzolla).

Fragrant petrol and diesel. Have you ever been stuck behind a diesel truck, belching diesel fumes? You wind up all the windows, but how do you breathe? Co-incidentally, the temperature in the pizza oven is the same as that inside the engine. So we should create an oil that, when burnt, gives off the aroma of freshly cooked pizza. This should be mixed with the diesel. Now everywhere the bus or the truck travels, it will leave a trail of pizza smell, rather than diesel fumes. Imagine the crows trying to locate the smell and pecking on the exhaust pipes! Pretty soon the diesel will come in varieties, such as pepperoni, meat lovers', vegetable supreme, etc. But let's not stop with the diesel. We can do the same for gasoline. Pretty soon we will see bumper stickers that say: "This car is powered by KFC BBQ Chicken!"

Fragrant Waste! Every year, the perfume factories throw away millions of gallons of perfume that was not quite the right formula, e.g. Chanel 9 ¾, if you get my meaning. Instead of throwing away all that stuff, why not use it in ways that will recover the cost or even make a profit? For example, toilet cleansers currently smell of chlorine (Ugh!). Why not of perfume? Or L'Oreal Toilet Duck? Or Givenchy Cleanser?

Pretty soon the toilet paper companies will get wind of this trend and we will see Yardley and Brut brand toilet paper instead of Charmin or Zeddy! The toilet paper would smell good, thereby relieving you of the duty to spray with air freshener. Now no one can accuse you of "stinking up the place". Soon, status designers will come out with designer toilet paper, with button–down versions. Question is, what would you button it to? (Don't even think of it!)

Are you laughing at these ideas? Remember, people laughed at Edison, Einstein and Wright Brothers too! Just think of the possibilities!

Flavoured Cigarettes. No matter how much you warn the public, people will smoke. Why not have have ingredients in the cigarette that do good, instead of harm? We already have menthol cigarettes, so why not other flavours? What we need are filters that screw on and off, so smokers can create their own varieties. These filters should be flavoured with things like:

Camphor, to relieve stuffed head and nose
Kosher Chicken Soup (don't ask!)
Cinnamon
Licorice

Undoubtedly, black marketers will come out with other flavours, such as marijuana, booze, etc., but that will only serve to make life more interesting!

Teeth Paint. Teeth contain enamel. So does paint. So, shouldn't you wash your walls with toothpaste? Of course, there are toxic substances in the paint, but remove them and we could use the paint on our teeth! We could get rid of yellow teeth simply by painting over! Now black teeth would be a matter of choice, not of neglect! We would even see people painting their teeth in different colours, stripes, designs, etc. Imagine a Smiley on someone's smile!

MODERN "BOY MEETS GIRL"

My wife decided to splurge her hard earned money on some Status cosmetics. We went to the exclusive store in Downtown Vancouver, and while she was getting a "free" makeover, I wandered about. I came to a perfume counter and saw that they now started making perfumes that smell like Grapefruit! I asked the sales clerk about this. She told me that that was the current craze among teenagers! Now I've been a teenager, my friend is a father of two teenagers, and let me tell you: The modern teenager is no different from the teenagers of yore. Teenage boys are not interested in girls at that awkward stage in their lives when their voices begin to change, hair erupts where there was none before, and they are rebelling against authority. No, the teenage boy is not interested in Musk by Jovan, but in Pizza by Gigi and chicken by barbecue. And in sports. Forget girls. Having established that as a fact, the industry should come out with perfumes that smell like pizza and barbecue chicken, or chocolate malt. Once the girl wears this, the teenage boys will follow her everywhere. Or to use sports to her advantage, the industry should come out with T-shirts that are receptive to satellite TV signal. At the tender age of 13, most girls' chests are relatively flat, so this should not cause a problem with the reception. The girl can activate the remote upon seeing the boy of her desires, and the remote would automatically beam the latest home team sports broadcasts. The boy would be watching the latest moves by his favourite sports hero on the girl's chest. The two could engage in conversation, and wherever the girl goes, the boy is likely to follow.

Those inventions are guaranteed to work better than Grapefruit perfumes! What would the grapefruit perfume do? Make you lose weight every time you wore it? Now there's something the industry can work on next!

FOR SALE

$\mathcal{M}$y wife and I were driving around and she saw a sign tacked to a telephone pole that said "For Sale"

It must have been a house for sale, as the other word was wrapped around the pole, so only the words "For Sale" were visible. My wife read the sign out loud, and said: "There's a house for sale". I looked at the sign and said: "No, that sign is on the post, so only the post is for sale." She said: "Oh."

Some time later, the penny dropped: "How can a telephone pole be for sale? Are you trying to fool me?"

I laughed so hard I was lost for a retort. She started laughing too, and remembered the time I played another trick on her. See the Three Wheeled Bicycle incident.

JUNKFOOD GALORE

As I write this article, the topic in the papers is how kids are getting fat by eating junk food in schools. Today's schools have vending machines that sell carbonated beverages, candies, and assorted junk food. So? When we Boomers were kids, we ate our share of junk food too, but the kids in our time never had obesity- related diseases such as diabetes and high blood pressure. So what was different?

I remember when we went to school, my parents would give me a couple of coins to spend on sweets and stuff. Sometimes, when Mom either forgot to pack my lunch, or simply did not have time to do so, my father would give me a $5 bill for lunch money. If we went to the canteen at the morning break with paper currency, the lady there would not accept it, and would refuse to serve us the candies, as she knew this was lunch money. After we had bought our lunch, if there were any coins left over, we could then spend that on the treats. In those days, you could buy things with pennies, and it was fairly easy to sneak out a couple of pennies now and again. We had gumball machines, but instead of gum, it contained peanuts. Today's kids can easily sneak out a couple of twonies, and they can buy much more stuff with that than we could with our couple of coins.

In those days, we did everything manually. We had to brush our teeth manually, mow the lawn by pushing the mower, and wash the dishes by hand. Today, we have battery-powered toothbrushes, dishwashers, and gas powered mowers that you can ride on! In those days, families had only one car, and the fathers used to take that to work. So when Mom needed groceries, she would send us kids to the nearest grocery store with the right amount of cash. Since there was no car, we had to walk to and from the store, and since there was not much cash left over, we could not really indulge in anything major.

Today, families have three cars, one for each parent, and one for the kids. Everyone takes the car even for small distances. Our modern lifestyle has virtually eliminated all forms of muscle flexing from our daily lives, except in the sports arena. No wonder today's kids are in the shape they are in! But don't blame only the junk food, blame rather the lifestyle. If we want changes in our kids' health, we will need to change the lifestyle, not just eating habits.

DIRECTOR OF FINANCE

When K learnt that his father had passed away in Tanzania, he had gone over to wind up the estate. On the way, he stopped by at Nairobi, and met with A at his place of work. A told K that the company had hired someone as director of finance who knew practically nothing about accounting, as he always had to refer to A as to how to do things. When K related the matter to me, I asked K what was his response to all this. K: "What could I say?"

Me: "You could have requested A to advise the director as follows. "Today, you are a Director of Five Naans: (Finance). If you do your work diligently, they may promote you to Director of Six Chapatis or even Seven Rotlas. But if you falter, you may be demoted to Director of Three Theplas or even Two Puris." "K laughed hard at this response of mine.

Note: Naans, chapattis, rotlas and puris are all varieties of Indian flat bread. Chapatis and rotlas are considerably bigger in size to theplas or puris.

HOT BANANA

When I was a kid, my parents would deposit me at my grandparents' house while they went out for the evening or weekend somewhere. She had a lot of fresh fruits in the house, and I used to enjoy eating the small variety of bananas. One day, she had not yet removed from the dining table the hot sauce from the evening meal. So, kids being kids, I added the hot sauce to the banana and ate it. YUMMY! I have loved that combination ever since, and whenever I get the chance, that's how I eat bananas now. When I went to Fiji to get married, my bride to be asked me what I wished to eat. I asked for banana and hot sauce. The banana I promptly received, but the hot sauce? They did not have anything remotely hot in that household. When I brought my wife here to Canada, I showed her how I eat the banana. She does not believe it to this day!

IKEA

When I was in Switzerland, we were given baseball caps bearing the name IKEA. We were told by the instructor that this was a famous Swedish furniture manufacturer. No one knew what the letters stood for, so I ventured a guess: Insurance Komapany of East Africa. Everyone laughed at this. Years later, when I was new to Canada, my parents, myself, my younger sister and my brother-in-law were in his car in Toronto, when he saw an IKEA store in the distance. He mentioned to my sister that they need to visit it soon. I challenged everyone to guess what the letters stood for. Me: "IKEA is obviously an acronym. Keep in mind it is a Swedish name, so there are bound to be some "glumps" and "flumps" in the name." My parents bowed out of the challenge, leaving my sister and brother-in-law with the anguish of figuring this one out. What must they be thinking as they tried to decipher the meaning? Sister: "How come he knows? He's only been in Canada one week and he knows? I've lived here over a decade and I still don't know!" Brother-in-law: "The cheek of this impudent fellow! Who does he think he is? Wait a minute. He must have seen the IKEA brochure lying around the house. Now, what did the fine print say?" When they finally gave up, I said: "Now let me see if I'm pronouncing this one properly. (PAUSE) Insurance Kompany of East Africa!" They roared with laughter, though I suspect my sister and her husband must have been mad at me for building up such a suspense for such a prank!

LITTLE THING

I work Sundays at a lottery booth, and to make things easier, there is usually, in every lottery booth, a separate machine that the customers can take their tickets to validate. This saves the clerk's time, as most tickets are not winners, so the customers can simply proceed to obtain new tickets, or go about their business. For two weeks, this little validating machine had been out of service. One old lady came up to me saying: "Your little thing is out of order. "I tried not to laugh, and proceeded to help other customers, until another customer in the queue piped up: "Yes, it needs a little Viagara. "I had no choice but to laugh, and the poor old lady turned crimson from embarrassment.

ALLERGIC REACTION

I worked at a warehouse for a few months. One day, the heavy metal door slipped and hit me on my head. The wound was superficial, but there was blood. So I was rushed to the nearest clinic. The doctor, after asking me the usual questions of name, address, etc. then proceeded to ask me if I was allergic to anything. I replied I was and his secretary was poised ready to write down my response. I stated I was allergic to "Income Tax and Photo radar." Both of them laughed at this. The doctor replied: "We all are."

GET WIND OF THIS

I have a habit of butchering songs. I put my own words to the familiar tunes, and the results are sometimes devastatingly funny. I did this to one of our hymns and sang my version to the landlady I stayed with. She laughed uncontrollably. A few days later, when she returned from prayers, she related to me the incident in the mosque that evening. It appears that they sang the same hymn that I chose to butcher. Whenever the congregation sang the chorus, she would recall my words and would start to giggle. The lead singer would therefore sing more verses, and every time the chorus came, the landlady would giggle some more. The more she giggled, the longer would be the hymn. The longer the hymn, the more numerous her giggles. After the service was over, someone asked her what was so funny. How could she tell them that her boarder had chosen to butcher the hymn they just sang? Everyone who hears my version laughs uncontrollably.

UP THE DOWN STAIRCASE

In my younger days, I would do almost anything on a dare. When I was in Atlanta, I used to date a sweet lady who was confined to a wheelchair. I had just got my new Mazda, and was showing off my new wheels to her. We went on several rides, and one day she dared me to do something stupid with the "new toy". She dared me to go wrong way on the highway. After midnight, the traffic in Atlanta in those days was almost non-existent, so this was easy for me. After making sure there were no cops around, I entered the highway from the exit and drove her home (about 15 miles) all the way. If someone was to stop me, I had a ready excuse. I was new to driving on the right hand side of the road, as back home we keep to the left. Since I was new to USA, this was as good as explanation as any. However, I did not need it. I was never caught. She was frightened all the way, as she could imagine a car coming at us the wrong way! Her knuckles had gone white from clutching the door grip so tightly, that she had a hard time letting go when we finally arrived at her door-step. She never dared me in anything after that.

EASY WHEN YOU KNOW

My friend from Toronto came to visit me in Surrey, BC. I was relatively new to the area, and I do not have a good sense of direction. Put the two together, and you have a perfect recipe for disaster. We went to visit a girl friend of his, and we were returning late in the evening. I decided to take the highway, as that would be faster, but I did not know what exit to get off at! So I guessed and got off at the wrong exit.

K asked me: "How can you get lost?"

Me: "Easy when you know!"

K: "It's even easier when you DON"T know!"

We laughed all the way home!

WALKING BACK HOME

During my boarding school days, we were given Saturday afternoons off. Most of the students decided to visit the nearby town for their leisurely pursuits, from dating, to seeing movies, smoking etc. The city bus used to be at our school compound at 2:00 PM and would leave in 15 minutes. The bus would be full as it headed to the town of Bridgewater. I was not interested in smoking, girls or anything like that. I used to go to the second hand store to buy used records of songs that had just gone off the charts. They would only cost 20% of the original price. So I could build up my collection very cheaply. Once I had bought what I wanted, I would head back to the school on foot. This gave me good exercise, I would see sights others would miss, meet interesting people, and get some fresh air while the others would be forced to inhale second-hand smoke in a crowded bus. I would sometimes stop by a bar (the British call them Pubs) and get a cool drink of shandy (beer mixed with Sprite). It is here that I got my nickname of Jamie, as the locals could never pronounce my given name. A group of adults with beer in their hands gathered around me. One of them asked the others: "What does he look like? Doesn't he look like a Peter?" They would cheer, drink, and someone else would offer another name, such as William. There would be a lot of whooping and beer guzzling. Along came a pretty but elderly woman who asked what was going on. When the men told her they were deciding on a name for me, she kissed me on the cheek and called me her "Darling Jamie!" Since then the name stuck.

I became friendly with a lot of the local folk there, and some of their humour must have rubbed off on me. Some people say that even today, I have a slight British accent! I would be the last to arrive back at the school, but was never punished for my tardiness, as the headmaster and the deputy both knew I was not up to any kind of mischief. I was merely socializing. The Headmaster was so impressed, that one day he took me for a ride on a single engine airplane, with him as the pilot. I got to see the countryside from a bird's perspective. Impressive! I got away with a lot that the others would have to answer for.

Rice, Curry, etc.

Back home there is a car dealership called Ryce Motors. So why not:
Curry Garage
Chapati Driving School
Lasi Auto Parts
Chutney Towing Service
Ladoo Car Wash
Halvah Car Rentals

FOREIGN ELEMENTS

The boarding school was renowned internationally. We had students from Africa (Kenya, South Africa, Zambia, Tanzania, Rhodesia), Europe (Czechoslovakia, France, Romania, Scandinavia), the Caribbean and USA. We also had a few local folks. These were the lucky ones. They would go home every week, and be with their families, and eat decent food for a change. In the beginning, the kids were from decent families, but as I was about to graduate, we had kids who were absolute hooligans. We had a group of local British boys who manipulated obtaining a driving licence. These four kids went on a driving rampage in a car they did not know how to handle. Needless to say, the car was wrecked, and all four of them died! Two of them were really smart and in the debate society with me. We had a French student who boasted of eating chocolate covered ants. He would let ants crawl up on his hands, and would proceed to lick them and eat them! The South African student was crazy for Golf. He would buy new golf clubs and go to practise his golf nearby every weekend. This was the time when Jack Nicklaus, Gary Player and Arnold Palmer were in the limelight. The student from Tanzania got involved in drugs and had to be expelled with his cohorts. The American students were really rowdy. They would destroy property. In one instance, one of the brothers jumped on a sink and used it as a urinal. Needless to say, these were also expelled. The student from Jamaica was crazy for Jimmy Hendrix and would pracitse loud music on his guitar. The one from Trinidad was an excellent soccer player. So what was I good at? Doing other people's homework and I was also in the church choir! Don't ask! This is where I learnt all kinds of Christian hymns, Christmas carols, etc.

Christmas time, if I did not have a place to go to (e.g. London with my relatives) there would be all kinds of festivities in the village. We went wassailing (singing Christmas carols and drinking hot wine or wassail), hay rides, tobogganing, had snowball fights, and everything else kids did in the winter.

The school's reputation dwindled after I left, and a couple of years later, it closed down.

EXTRA CURRICULAR ACTIVITIES

I was not, and am not, much into sports. The Headmaster decided that every one must indulge in some sort of extracurricular activity. There were all kinds of activities going on, for the students to choose and participate. I had an avid stamp collection, so for a while I joined the philatelic club. It got to be boring so I left after a couple of terms. I joined the debating society and learnt to think on my feet. This was something I was good at. I also had a good voice, so I was inducted into the school's choir. Every Christmas or Easter, there would be various presentations by the students. Our Choirmaster was the Chemistry teacher, who was half-deaf. (We played a lot of pranks in his class as he droned on and scribbled on the blackboard. He hadn't the slightest idea what we were up to! In one instance, a bee landed near the workbench, so I grabbed it by the tweezers, and shoved in into a test tube. I then poured acid, and the thing gave off a stink as it decomposed. Mr. Ettridge was not the slightest bit aware). We had modeling classes. The kids would build model airplanes, boats, etc., fit them with engines and fly / sail them. One student decided on a remote control version. He built it with his own hands, did everything right, and we saw him fly it a few times. The last time he went to fly it, it never came back. Someone else had a stronger control, and "stole' that plane from him! I could not do much with my hands, as I found out in the carpentry classes, so I quit that. I did take up piano lessons, and the instructor would invite me over to her home for dinner sometimes. I would join her family in the evening meals and would enjoy the classical music she would play on the piano. Since I came from a musical family, this was a breeze for me.

Other activities I enjoyed were go-kart racing. Students who were new to driving got to ride on go-karts that only had one speed; more experienced drivers would get on those that had gears. This is where I developed my love for driving. We would drive around the back parking lot, and would be supervised by at least two instructors. Both of them were brothers of the headmaster. These brothers also taught carpentry, working with clay, maths, technical drawing and PE. I could never make anything worthwhile with the clay because of my clumsy hands. But it opened my eyes to all the crafts.

FIELD TRIPS

At least twice in a year, the school would organize field trips. I remember visiting a dairy farm. We saw how cows are milked, how butter and cheese are made, and basically had an educational but fun filled day. The school had to hire three or more busses that would take the kids and the staff to the various locations. The kitchen was busy preparing lunch bags for everyone. Sandwiches, fruit, sometimes cold Yorkshire pudding. We also visited Cheddar Gorge, famous for cheddar cheese. We were given free samples of the cheeses on the trip.

We also visited nearby islands where we saw puffins aplenty; holiday resorts such as Butlin's, and a few fun fairs. Our Geography teacher decided one day to take her class to her husband's farm for the day. There we could see all the activities of a farm and get some insight into agriculture. She had a lot of cows, so we saw the cows being milked again; near her house she had a fruit garden and strawberries were in season. We ate ourselves silly! The part I did NOT like was the stink caused by the manure. They would accumulate all the cow droppings for use later as fertilizer. The stench was overwhelming for city kids like us! I held my nose most of the time we were outdoors, and the instructor looked at me in disapproval, but what to do? How can anyone breathe with such stench? This time, the lunch was a treat. All the food was grown fresh on the farm. No sandwiches for us that day! I filled my belly with the delicious roast beef, brussels sprouts, potatoes, gravy, and of course, strawberries and farm fresh cream!

We then had to write reports on the various filed trips when we returned to school.

DRINKING AND SMOKING

$\mathcal{M}$y father was an avid drinker, so there was always booze free flowing in the house. My father preferred beer, whisky, and other hard stuff; my mother preferred sherry and sweet wines, whilst my uncles preferred gin, vodka and rum. I tried my father's beer once and found it distasteful at that age, but I loved mother's sherry. Whenever my father would call his friends to play cards, I would sneak a few sips of my mother's sherry. I was so naughty, they decided to teach me the games and I became quite good at these.

My father also started smoking, and he went with Benson and Hedges. I saw a packet lying around when he had gone to work, so my friend and I decided to sneak one out and light up. Neither he nor myself enjoyed the experience, so we never touched cigarettes again.

In school, the kids would sneak off to the woods to light up. One day I passed by and one student grabbed me, and practically forced me to take a smoke. These kids smoked the macho brands like No. 6, not the sissy brands like my father. And these cigarettes had no filter! Yuck! I took one whiff and that was it. No more smokes for me from that day onwards, or so I thought.

When I was in Atlanta, the big thing there then was pot. My friends would light up, and beg me to take a couple of whiffs. I did, but it had no effect on me except I became hungry! Whilst my friends were enjoying the highs produced by the experience, I used to stare at them dumbfounded. One even had the audacity to tell me: "Jamie, you are a waste!" meaning that it was no use spending money to try to get me high. I never asked for help in that direction, so their complaints were unfounded.

One Christmas, we kids from Africa were left stranded at school. The holidays were too short to justify travel back to Africa, and for one reason or another, we could not visit our friends / relatives in nearby cities. Since we were stuck in the same place for a few days, what to do? My friend's elder brother was of legal age, so he would buy all sorts of booze and cigarettes from the village store, while we who were not yet of age would buy the snacks and the soft drinks. We would get back to the school, go to his room, play music eat and drink. This one student from Zambia decided to eat the bite-sized snacks without chewing them! When he mixed the different drinks and got sick, he threw up right in the middle of the floor. We saw the biscuits still whole lying on the floor. Someone had to mop up the mess, and at 3:00 AM, we finally decided to get some sleep. We never had such a drunken party again.

I continued to drink sherry, sweet wines and beer once in a while in Atlanta. When I returned to Kenya, I gave up booze after a couple of years, and have never touched it again.

THE POWER OF PRAYER

I am not very religious, as I mentioned previously. But I have found that whenever I pray for the good of the community (as opposed to ego needs) the prayers are almost always answered. Examples:

I saw on TV one day that the RCMP was looking for certain criminals. When the RCMP have to make an appeal to the public, they need help! Who better to help than Almighty God? So when I prayed, I also asked for these criminals to be caught. Guess what? One week later, as I was ironing my clothes and glimpsing at the TV occasionally, I saw that these criminals had finally been caught!

In Victoria, one summer there was a situation of water rationing. Now, how can a city by the sea, in a country like Canada, in the dawn of the 21st century, have water shortage problems? I wrote a stinking letter to the local paper, which they did not have guts to print. But I also prayed to God for rain. One week later it rained steadily, so much so that the water ban was lifted for the rest of that summer.

We are too absorbed in "ME FIRST" that we lose sight of the communal good. Perhaps if we prayed for the betterment of the community, half the problems would disappear and we could get on with our lives in peace and harmony.

UP ON THE ROOF

My mother swears the following stories about me are true. I have no recollection of these, so make of them what you will:

I was enrolled at a nursery school (kindergarten) at a tender age of three. I am supposed to have sneaked out of the main room while the rest of the kids were asleep (taking naps after lunch) and took all their shoes and threw them on the roof. A kid aged three cannot have the muscle power to throw anything that high, so the story smacks of innuendo.

I am also supposed to have sat, at primary school, behind a girl who had her hair in braids. I am supposed to have taken a pair of scissors and cut off one of those braids, leaving her hair lop-sided. If that story is true, did the girl not feel anything tugging at her hair? When my father heard this story, he merely laughed, instead of disciplining me. Why, if the event was true, was I not punished? Again, how credible are these stories?

HOME COOKING

My father was a violent man. After bringing two kids into this world, my elder sister and myself, he still could not tolerate my mother's cooking. If anything was prepared not quite to his taste, he would throw that plate of food upon the wall, scream at my mother, and eat out. My mother would be in tears. So when she was pregnant with my younger sister, my mother obviously could not and would not cook. So my father made arrangement with a hotel downtown for them to provide, on a monthly basis, food to go. He would pick up the food on his way home, and we would eat that for supper and next day for lunch. Breakfast was usually cereals, eggs, toast and tea, so these were never any problem. We ate this food well past my mother's delivery. That hotel has since been torn down, the road renamed, and the downtown landscape has changed substantially over the years.

PICNIC TIME

At least one Sunday per month, my father would organize a mass picnic at a secluded spot not too far from the city. He would ring up his friends. Their wives would prepare the food, the men would bring booze and musical instruments, and we would all head on out to Mua Hills. This spot had a stream running by a pasture of land. This place was normally unoccupied, so we would spread out the bed sheets on the grass, and the food, booze, musical instruments would be arranged on this. The women would be busy preparing the food, the kids would be playing nearby, and the men would be busy getting drunk and someone would provide musical entertainment. By the time we were ready to eat, the adult men would be thoroughly drunk, the women upset at men's behaviour, the food piping hot, and the kids already fed and some of them would have dozed off to sleep. Thank God there were a couple of sober adults who would then arrange to drive the rest of the troupe home. While we were reveling in all this, the local kids would wander nearby and take a peek at our frivolities. They would take all the left over food, so we never had a problem disposing of the excess. The left over booze, however, would be carefully packed into the cars. This went on for years, until one fine day, the local jam manufacturer bought out the land and converted that land into a factory. So our picnics were then moved to the back yard. My father had a huge back yard, and he would bring from the factory a couple of tents. In this area would the frivolities begin. My cousin was now old enough to be married. He made a fool of himself at one of these parties, and my mother never forgave him for it. I was too young to remember all the details. A couple of years after that, my father's brothers began to emigrate to Canada and England, so the picnics came to a sudden halt. Soon, my father also left Kenya for good, and settled in England. My two sisters and myself are now settled in Canada. My parents are in England with my younger brother and his family.

HOW DO YOU LIKE YOUR COFFEE?

When K was here visiting me, we met a mutual friend who also used to work for the same company back in Kenya. While they were catching up on their gossip, I interjected:

"You know, pretty soon it will be time for K to get married and settle down. When he does get married, I suggest that one of his sisters take a photograph of him with a mug of coffee in his hands. He should be flanked, on one side, by his wife and the other side, by his other sister. We could caption the photograph:

COFFEE AND KARIM WITH TWO SUGARS." They all laughed at this.

LEARNING TO DRIVE

Once I returned from boarding school, I had time on my hands. I decided I would learn how to drive, after the go-kart activities sparked the fire of driving in me. I was enrolled at a local driving school, and to give me practice, my father employed a chauffeur to be with me whenever I went anywhere. I had the free use of my mother's car most of the time, so the chauffeur and I would head on out to some country roads and I would practice my driving. I used to drive slowly and cautiously in the beginning, but after I obtained my driving licence, I would dare to drive faster than the dull 30 MPH. For this, my chauffeur and I would travel towards Thika, Naivasha, or other nearby towns, on roads that were at that time of the day, not too busy. There were times when my mother would need the car, so my father decided to give me one that was being driven by one of my cousins as he went overseas to study. So now I had a sporty car that really flew! I was also made to work at my father's factory, so then the chauffeur would be with my mother. He had plenty of time on his hands, so periodically he would take the car "to get filled" or so we were told. My father noticed that for the amount of miles on the car, the fuel bill was excessive. He put a detective on the case, and we discovered that the chauffeur was siphoning the fuel out of the car to sell to his friends. So he was soon fired. Now I could drive around without a chauffeur. So obviously mother made me do all the errands. I was one day asked to pick up my sister and her friend from a spot downtown and bring the two home. My habit was to race along at a decent clip, but my sister thought that was too fast, so she repeatedly asked me to slow down. I did slow down a few times, only to race again. This time my sister screamed at me to slow down, so I decided I would indeed slow down. I never shifted out of first gear. We arrived home two hours late, and everyone was worried where we were. There were no cell phones in those days, so there was no way to keep in touch whilst mobile. I explained to my parents that I was merely going slow, but my mother said I was going TOO slow! You can't please everyone!

BUYING POWER

*B*ack in my Atlanta days, this was the era of Nixon and the Price Freeze. Before Watergate. People were looking for ways to save money. The farmers would bring their produce to a nearby town at a Farmer's Market, but the fools would only sell in large quantities. How many pounds of apples can a single person buy? Or potatoes? Or cabbage? The prices were indeed cheap, but we had to buy in large quantities. So I made friends with neighbours and we organized a Buying Committee. Each week, someone different would be given a list of what to buy and how much. When he / she returned, we would divide up the purchases and the cost. Someone always had a pair of scales, so it was very easy to measure out and divide equitably. This worked until someone moved or dropped out, and new members were inducted. This was also the era of Cash and Carry where the merchants would simply leave everything in boxes. We had to remove from the boxes what we wanted, and had to price everything by hand. No bar codes in those days. There would be pieces of chalk on every aisle, and we had to mark the price and minimum quantity on the purchase. This worked fine for canned goods, since such food did not spoil so it was cheaper to buy in large amounts. But how about perishables, such as milk? With time, the price advantage disappeared, and the concept shared the fate of the hula burger and promptly died. Then came the big boxes and Costco. In large cities such as London, such Co-operative stores may still be flourishing, but in comparatively smaller cities, these are now as rare as pink diamonds.

WHAT MEMORY!

When K was on his way to Kenya and Tanzania, I asked him if he knew anyone there by the name of Damji Giga. He said that that family had mostly left the country, but there might still be someone here and there. So I asked him to conduct this experiment. He must go up to someone from the Giga family with a floppy diskette and ask that person to bite thee times anywhere on the floppy. If the person hesitated, K was supposed to demonstrate, that there was nothing dangerous about it. When the friend complied, he could proudly claim: "See, it's only a floppy, but it has three Giga bites!" K laughed when he heard this but he did not have the nerve to carry out the ploy.

SNAKES IN OUR BACKYARD

*B*efore independence, Kenya was a highly racist country, with the areas pretty well defined for Whites, Asians and local Blacks. Asians could not live in the White neighborhoods. But after independence, all this changed. My father decided to move to the White area of town. We bought the house on the corner of Ring Road Parklands and Westlands Avenue, in Nairobi. The house came with a huge garden of 1 ¼ acres. The property was fenced, for a very genuine reason. The unfenced area was wilderness, and from there snakes would enter our property. The first time this happened, our servants got frightened and ran after the snake with a panga, a machete-like tool. When my father heard about it, he made some enquiries. He was told that the next time that happened, to call up the local Museum, and they would capture the snake live. We were given $50 for each snake captured, as an incentive. Over the years, the Museum must have captured no less than 20 snakes from our back yard. Most of these were pythons, which crush their prey before eating them. An adult python can easily devour an entire sheep in one meal. But that snake would not feel hungry again for days. We could see the snakes at the snake pit at the museum, and whenever someone came from overseas, we would take them to the Museum as one of their sightseeing spots. As the years progressed, most of Westlands was taken over by the Asian community. The wilderness soon was a matter of history, as the area became developed to accommodate more of the emerging affluent class. The place where the snakes roamed free and made their home, now accommodates a Hindu temple and social hall!

CROOKED STEEPLE

While I was in Boarding school, one summer my parents decided to visit me in England. So I stayed at my uncle's house and when my parents arrived, they stayed at another one of my uncle's house. My mother decided to cook something. The oven in that house was gas powered, and my mother was not used to cooking on a gas range. Nevertheless, she decided to put something in the oven and proceeded to take her bath while the food cooked. When she emerged from the bath in her robe, she opened the oven door to see what was the progress. Since she had not bothered to light the oven, the gas had accumulated, and when the door opened, it ignited on one of the pilot lights and she got burnt. There was a loud bang in the process, and my father just walked in after buying a newspaper. He finally managed to put out the flames but my mother was badly scarred, her hair singed. I got a phone call from my father asking me what to do when a person got burnt, and my training at St. John's Ambulance paid off. I advised him what to do. He took my mother to the doctor, who gave her some medications. The burns were superficial, but the scars would take time to go away.

This made my mother very shy to meet people, so my father and uncles decided we could take a visit outside of London for a few days. Where to go? Finally, they decided on The Lake District, north of London. This area is famous for lakes caused by the glaciers, and is the home area of poets such as Wordsworth and Colleridge and home of The Potteries, where Wedgwood china comes from. We saw the lakes called Buttermere, Windermere, and other meres. Mere means lake. We saw a church with a crooked steeple. It was straight at one time, but I forgot the explanation the locals gave. Maybe it was caused by a fierce storm. My mother was enjoying all this, though she was all covered up like a proper Muslim woman, in order to hide the ugly scars. We went on numerous boat rides, enjoyed the local cuisine and enjoyed the splendor of Mother Nature in her pristine beauty. When I went back to school, I had plenty to write about how I spent my summer holidays. Thank God that gas ovens have now become automated and would never allow this kind of tragedy to be repeated.

PET PEEVE

The difference in ages between my younger sister and myself is seven years, and between myself and my younger brother about 12 years. So I never had a companion to play with. So most of my life I spent with pets. This started out innocently by buying a rabbit on the country roads, and we added to this another rabbit, some chickens, a parrot and a dog. The chickens served a useful purpose: they provided us with eggs. We had built a chicken coop, and the rabbits stayed on one side, and the chickens in another. We would let the chickens out occasionally, but all was fenced in, so they could wander in a limited area only. This gave them exercise.

The first dog I had, my father bought from an animal hospital. The poor dog had a broken leg and was abandoned by its previous owners. The dog would walk with a limp, but it became so bad that finally it had to be put down. It could not run and play with me, so that defeated the purpose of having a dog in the first place. The next dog we had was an Alsatian puppy, black and brown. This is one I could play with, and I did. We romped about and gave each other exercise.

We also had an Indian parrot, green with red beak. It could not speak, and try as we might, refused to learn to speak. It could whistle a few tunes. We thought that his wings were clipped, so we never paid much attention every time we cleaned the cage. Twice it flew off, but was within the house so we managed to recapture it. Still, my parent s did not wise up and have its wings clipped, and finally it flew away.

My younger brother was developing asthma, and the doctor thought this was due to the pets, so all my pets were given away when I was in boarding school. Later, when my family moved to England, they found out it was not asthma, but that he was allergic to milk. He quit drinking milk and eating dairy products, and his troubles vanished. So my pets became the scapegoats needlessly.

EYE OF THE BEHOLDER

My grandmother lived in a home with a lovely garden in the front. Here, she must have planted a few herbs such as cilantro and hot peppers. My younger sister and I were left at my grandmother's place whilst my parents and elder sister went to town. My sister dressed up as a teacher, as was her habit and pretended to teach a make-believe class of students. She soon tired of this, and went outdoors. There she must have touched the pepper tree, and something must have gotten into her eye. Without thinking, she rubbed her eye with the hand that previously had touched the pepper tree. We heard a loud scream. Immediately, I was blamed for her misfortune, only for them to realize that I was indoors and she was outdoors. The servant brought her in, and my grandmother proceeded to clean her eye with water and cold milk. All this time, her screams got louder and she swore she would die! I got the scolding for something I did not do. In between my sister's sobs, she managed to tell us what happened. My aunt and grandmother forgave me for something I did not do. Eventually, the pain subsided and the redness in her eye was gone. But during those few hours, she lived through Hell!

AM I READING THIS RIGHT?

I am always amazed at the signs people put up. What they intend to say and what is actually said are not always the same. In Nairobi, at one of the residential compounds, was the sign that read: "Watch Out for Children." Boy, those kids must be terrors! How about another one that read: "Slow. Children." No need to tell us, enroll them in special school! I bet what these signs DID wish to convey was: "Caution. Children at play." But the way these signs were worded, gave totally different meanings.

HOLD MAMA'S HANDS

I would not have believed it if I had not seen this with my own eyes. As I stopped at a traffic light, I saw a mother duck with her brood in tow, crossing at the crosswalk! How did the duck know where to cross and when to cross the road? After the lights had turned green, the motorists were reluctant to move, as they were totally awe struck by the intelligence of Mother Nature's creatures!

CAR RENTAL BUSINESS

I used to rent out cars when I was still a teenager, in boarding school. Not the real cars, but electric racing cars. I made enough money doing other people's homework, and washing dishes that I could now afford to splurge. I bought a model racing car set, that my friend Mark helped me to assemble. We raced each other, and passers-by would stop to investigate the cause of all the noise. Pretty soon, every one wanted to try it out, so I saw this as a business opportunity and charged the fellow students one penny for 10 laps. In those days, money had value. This was the era of John Kennedy as President. We saw the tragedy of his assassination on TV. The British system then was pounds, shillings and pence. Twelve pennies made one shilling, and twenty shillings made one pound. At the prevailing exchange rate then, one British penny was roughly equal to one American or Canadian penny. With one penny, then, you could buy a couple of sticks of bubble gum, or weigh yourself on one of the scales in front of many shops. A bus ride from our school into town was thee pence. A brand new single on vinyl cost eight shillings, or just about one dollar. A second hand record cost half crown, or two shillings and six pence, or thirty pennies. With the money I made on the car rental business, I then purchased a model train set. Now there was not enough space for both the train and the car set, so the car set was put away as the train set was assembled. But the train was too slow, no excitement, so it was not popular. So the train set got put away for good, and the car racing set dominated the scene. Ultimately, both these sets ended up at my father's house in London, where by younger brother played whilst I studied in Atlanta.

Most of the kids would get pocket money or allowance of a half crown (30 pennies) every week, I had an allowance of double that amount, or five shillings per week. The rich kids would get an allowance of ten shillings or even one pound per week. All this was of course, payable by our parents with the fees. In a previous chapter, I mentioned dollars, instead of shillings, so that the readers would get an idea of the cost in today's terms, but these were in shillings, not dollars.

WATER, WATER EVERYWHERE

What irks me the most, is that in Canada, in two cities by the sea, on the dawn of the twenty-first century, there is shortage of water! I wrote to the papers when I was in Victoria, but they did not have the guts to publish my letter. When I moved to Vancouver, I wrote to the papers here, seven years later, and my letter received prominence in the letters page. It was all boxed up, and the headline was bold. Basically, I wrote to the papers saying that it is understandable that water shortage crises would occur in a third-world country, or in a land-locked country, but in Canada, with all the modern technology at its disposal, in two major cities by the sea, this problem was absolutely inexcusable! I also suggested ways they could alleviate the situation such as:

Seeding the clouds. By seeding the clouds with silver dioxide, this could cause the rains to fall. There are plenty of overcast days here in the Lower Mainland and in Victoria, so why not make use of the technology at our disposal? The rains would not only water the lawns, but also raise the water level in the dams.

Build dams in certain areas that are prone to floods. This makes too much sense, therefore the politicians would not do it. But if the flood-prone areas, such as The Malahat in Vancouver Island, had dams built there, this would not only be relief from the flood, but also increase the water supply in times of need.

Desalination. This is too easy. Desalinate the seawater. If the desalination plant at or around the beach area is a problem, simply pump the water to another area of town and desalinate from there. If the station were solar-powered, this would also help to conserve energy, and provide us with water in the season when we need it the most, i.e. summertime!

Re-channel rain water. Right now, the rain water ends up in the drains and that water ends up in the sea. What good is that? The water from the drains could be re-routed and pumped back into the dams, thereby increasing the water level even faster.

Separate potable water from non-potable water. Currently, all the water that comes into the households and businesses is ready to drink, i.e. potable. We use the same water to flush the toilet, water the lawn, mop the floor and cooking. If only the water that came into the kitchens was potable, we could use non-potable water for other chores, as is the practice in other parts of the world. This would save millions in water treatment costs, as our lawns do not need fluoride treated water.

Two years after my letter appeared, we still have water rationing in Canada!

MONTHLY CURSE

I've dated many women in my time, and a few of them suffered intensely during their monthlies. One of them even said to me "You'll never know what it's like!" True, I never could imagine the exact same thing happening to me. But I could sympathize, as I also suffered from a monthly curse: Ingrown toenail! One woman in particular suffered cramps and could not walk for a day or two. Well, with my problem, I suffered the same consequence. If I did not remove the ingrown toenail, it would start digging into the inside flesh of my toe, causing me enormous pain. I could not walk. If I did manage to pull it out, by using toenail clippers and a nail file to lift the offending culprit, the toe would normally swell up, causing me pain for a few days. So the consequences were the same whether I removed the ingrown toenail or not. I could not walk properly. At times the pain has gotten to be so bad, that even if a bed sheet lay on the offending toe, it would throb in pain. After maybe five days, the pain would go away, and the procedure had to be repeated once a month. I've had this problem since my teens, and remains to this date.

PORT OF PEACE

$\mathcal{B}$efore 1961, the three countries now called Kenya, Uganda and Tanzania were one community, called East Africa. True, these were separate countries back then too, but there was much free flow of goods and services, almost like provinces within a larger country. Zanzibar was a separate island and after Tanganyika became independent in 1961, Zanzibar was absorbed by Tanganyika and the country was renamed Tanzania. In those days, British Airways was British Overseas Airways Corporation, or BOAC for short. East Africa had its own communal airline called East African Airways. The railroad system was East African Railways and Harbours.

My father had two brothers, so the main branch of the company was in Nairobi. My father and his elder brother looked after it. The middle brother looked after the branch in the capital city of Tanganyika, Dar Es Salaam, which is Arabic for "Port of Peace". Whenever my uncle in Tanganyika wanted to go on vacation, my father would be summoned to run the Dar Es Salaam branch. So my father would dutifully pack up the family for a few weeks / months and we would be off to Dar. For a while, maybe two or three days, my uncle and his family lived with my father and his family in the small flat. We would be shown where everything was, he would hand over the keys to my father, and if this was still during the school year, the kids would be enrolled in Aga Khan Primary School nearby for the duration of the school term. Then my uncle and his family would depart, leaving the flat to my father.

Dar is just about on the equator, at sea level, so it was stifling hot most of the time there. In those days there were no such things as air conditioning, so most houses and businesses had fans. All the loose papers and cloths had to be weighted down, or they would fly off hither and yon. I used to complain that it was so hot, but my mother put an end to all my complaints by saying: "This is practice for you when you end up in Hell!" or words to that effect. Imagine such words coming out of the mouth of a mother!

My younger sister was just about one or two years old. My uncle had three daughters and one son. All of them lived in a flat (apartment) on the second or third floor of a building. The bottom floor had shops. I used to frequent one grocery store there that had the most delicious commercially available mango ice cream! This used to be pop sickle style, but ice cream! From the balcony of his flat, I could almost reach out and pluck the fruit of the bitter almond tree. This was called "Khungu" in Swahili. The fruit was about the size of one or two grapefruits, but oval in shape. There was very little flesh, all maroon in colour when ripe, about 2 millimeters thick on a shell that housed the bitter almonds. The flesh was dry but deliciously sweet! The shell had to be cracked open to reveal the almonds inside. We as kids were not interested in the bitter almonds inside, so we were only concerned with the outside flesh. Because there was not much flesh to the large fruit, any card hand dealt that was almost worthless was also dubbed to be Khungu. So was anyone who did not have much common sense or intelligence.

We had lychees (shokay shokay) aplenty, as they came from Zanzibar. There were two varieties, but the ones that were the sweetest were black when ripe. The dark red varieties were not as sweet. These were also plentiful in our little flat. At school, or on the way from school, we used to eat kitale. This is young coconut, with the outer shell shaved, revealing the tender flesh that housed the coconut water. The water was sweet, but if we drank everything, we could not eat the kitale, so we used to spill most of the water. The empty shell was now filled with pieces of potatoes that were boiled, sprinkled with salt and paprika. Eaten with the coconut flesh, this was almost a taste of heaven! I used to skimp on my lunch at school so that I could enjoy this treat! We did not get kitales in Nairobi, so I made the most of whatever opportunities I had while in Dar.

Another fruit that we enjoyed in Dar but not readily available in Nairobi was Hoka. This was a dry fruit, about the size of a cricket ball, and reddish-orange in colour. The outer layer had to be peeled off, revealing a yellow mass that was stringy but very sweet. Since there was not much juice to it, most of it would get stuck to our teeth. But the experience was worth it!

We also ate our share of cassava, roasted and sprinkled with salt and paprika, sweet potatoes also prepared the same way, but we could get these in Nairobi also, so this was not really something we looked forward to while in Dar.

At least once every two years, my father would visit Dar with the family so that my uncle could take a long deserved vacation. This continued until one fine day, the Tanzania president decided to make the country communist and started nationalizing everything. My uncle migrated to Kenya. He bought a condominium at Forces Lane, the previous home of the pythons. There were music parties a plenty in my father's back yard, as I mentioned elsewhere in this book.

My father's eldest brother was a diabetic, and being elderly, was semi-retired. He therefore could not be summoned to run the Dar branch by himself, which is why we never had a branch in Uganda, another neighbouring country to Kenya. It was this uncle's younger son that made a fool of himself at the party. It was also this cousin that had a heart attack before reaching 30 years of age. He used to drink sodas and eat fatty foods that quickly raised his cholesterol level to a danger zone. We visited him in hospital, and hopefully he has modified his habits over the years.

CHILDHOOD FRIENDS

Today's lives are highly mobile, with people leaving one city or even one country for another. It is therefore no surprise that many of my childhood friends are no longer in Kenya, but have scattered with the wind. When I was working for the electronics retailer, for a while I was posted at the store in North Vancouver. One day this old lady came to the store asking for directions to some place. I recognized her straight away, and asked her how her sons were doing. I introduced myself to her, and she was amazed I could recognize her after so many years. We lived in one half of the duplex owned by her husband, and she and her family lived in the other half. She had two sons, the elder of whom was younger to me, called Aftab, which is Arabic for "Sunshine". The younger was Altaf. She also had two daughters, Fatima and Najma. She lived with the elder daughter, Najma in North Vancouver.

Her husband used to be a carpenter, and he was a master of his trade. So much so, that the Royal Family would place orders at his business for anything they needed, and when Kenya became independent in 1963, the throne for the President was also ordered from his business. They even have a public garden named after the family, and the name remains to this day.

I remember the house had a long driveway. On the border of the driveway, were all kinds of fruit trees, including guavas, loquat (a sweet yellow fruit), mulberries, and elsewhere in the property they had trees of banana, apple, raspberries, gooseberries, and pomegranates.

We used to climb the trees, and play there, and also eat the fruit. We ate ourselves silly with the fruits in season.

She gave me the addresses of her sons in England. I wrote to both of them, but they never replied my letters. I reminded them that we used to live in that house, and our misadventures together, but I guess both the brothers are too busy with their families to worry about the friends from their past.

I ran into some other friends in Nairobi, when I used to work for the Insurance company, and they too gave me their Canadian addresses, and when I moved here, I wrote to them, but no response.

The only ones that have kept in touch are the ones I have written about in this book, G, K, F and a couple of others.

LOCAL BUSINESSMAN MAKES GOOD

I read in one of the British papers that a prominent businessman had recently died, and the estate was to be split up amongst his various children. The daughters were left out in the will, and they too wanted a share. He migrated form Kenya to England. We used to eat at his restaurant. This was before independence, in a run down section of Nairobi, on River Road, on the second floor, was Patak's restaurant. The food was traditional Indian fare, served on a metal plate called "Thali".

The food was totally vegetarian. There would be servers roaming around the floor with fresh food, chapattis, curries, and if they saw someone with meager food on his / her thali, they would automatically add more to the thali. We had to refuse any more helpings if we were full. After independence, this family left Kenya during the exodus. He started a similar restaurant in London, but because there was no one to supply the condiments and the chutneys, her made his own. The customers would ask him where they could buy these condiments, and soon he started selling these from his restaurant. The sideline proved to be more profitable than the restaurant, so the restaurant was sold off, and he started a factory making these condiments. These are now exported worldwide.

PIZZA TIME!

One of my jobs during my Atlanta years, was at a local Pizza parlour. As Management Trainee, I had to learn the business from the ground up. One of my various duties was to cut all the ingredients for the pizza (e.g. onions, green peppers, etc.) and keep these ready for the day. I also had to make the dough, for the two kinds of crusts, the regular and thick crust. I would never know how much to prepare, but if something were left over, it would have to be used up the very next day. So I had to listen to the news on the local radio station. If there was a ball game at the nearby locations, there could be a large crowd in the evening. Thank God our store was a family store, so we did not serve beer at that location. At the other branches, with the beer flowing so freely, the customers would get rowdy and many times the manager would have to break up fights. I would have to be at the kitchen at least before 10:00 AM, to prepare for the lunch crowd, and then for the evening crowd. The manager at that location would generate extra business by having luncheon buffets. All you can eat, for a set price. WE, the staff would decide what ingredients we would put on the pizza, and the customer could then pick and choose the slices to his / her satisfaction. There would never be more than three ingredients on any one pizza, but there would be a whole variety to select, from single ingredient pepperoni to vegetarian, to meat lover's delight. I loved the jalapenos, so I made sure that this appeared on at least two pizzas. Whatever pizza was left over, we, the staff could eat. (We also got, as part of our pay, one free small size pizza per shift. So if we worked a double shift, we could take home a large size pizza, compliments, which I did many times). Since most of the people did not care for jalapeno, I used to eat all the left over pizzas with jalapeno, plus I would take home my free pizza. This is probably where I acquired my middle age spread, which refuses to subside to this day. If I felt naughty on any one particular day, I would cover the ingredients with the cheese on top, so that the customers never knew what they were biting into! These were guaranteed to contain jalapeno.

WHAT'S IN A NAME?

*P*lenty, if it is original. What annoys my parents the most is lack of originality in naming the children. When my elder sister was born, my maternal grandmother picked out a few names from the Koran, my mother's sister mentioned a few names, these were then written down, and my parents chose one from that list. Soon after she was named, anyone in our community who had a daughter, also started naming their children the same as my sister's name, or a variation of it! This thoroughly disgusted my father, not realizing that imitation is the sincerest form of flattery. In his younger and violent days, he said a few things to a few families. When I came along, my paternal grandfather was so overjoyed at the prospect of a grandson, that he promptly registered my name at the city hall. When my mother came home from hospital, she was aghast at the name my grandfather had given me, so she renamed me. At the community register, my name is what my mother preferred. So the name on my passport is different from the name on my birth certificate. Soon after my birth, most boys born in the community had a name similar to mine! Then came along my younger sister, with a profusion of girls in the community bearing her name as well. Needless to say, the same scenario is repeated with the naming of my younger brother.

When I was doing my practicum for the insurance, I worked at an agency owned by someone from our community. I overheard one of the brothers discussing children's names. When I enquired, I was given the explanation that the names in that family were unique. None of the uncles or aunts had children with the same names. If anyone in the extended family decided to name one of their newborn with a name they had decided, they would select an alternate name, so that there were never any duplicates. One of the brothers was a walking dictionary on Muslim names. He could tell you the meaning of the name, and famous personalities with that name, what made them famous, etc. Who cares? Just let me work in peace!

INTRODUCTION TO THE COMPUTER

When I was working for the Insurance Company in Nairobi, not many desks had computers. A co-worker showed me the basics, so I got the hang of it pretty fast. Then I got transferred to the Pensions Department. Here, they have to prepare a schedule showing contributions made by the employee, the employer, interest earned on the contributions, and the expected future value at the present growth rate. This gets to be tedious if done manually, so I devised a way for the computer to do this. I got it to print on the standard computer paper, and voila! Soon, some clerk asked me if I could "introduce "him to the computer. I am supposed to have done the following, but I have absolutely no recollection of it: I am supposed to have taken the clerk to a place where there was a work station, asked him to stand a few feet back, and "introduce" him to the computer by saying: "Clerk, this is computer. Computer, this is Clerk." Other staff members swear this story is true, and it is probably something I would do. But I have no recollection of the alleged event. That clerk now works in the Pensions Department, and is fairly proficient in using the computer.

THE PAST IS THE FUTURE

Have you noticed all the toys we played with as kids are now coming back? Toys such as Hula-hoops were the craze in the sixties, and they are back again. So were yo-yos, scooters, Slinkies, superballs, and a whole host of others that the kids play with now. The same is true for fashion. The designers have run out of creative ideas, so the clothes of decades past are making a comeback. What is most annoying is that songs are re-released by someone else, in a version that is butchered and we are supposed to like it? Songs such as "Far Away" originally sung by Carole King are now sung by groups that do not do justice to the song. If you have not heard the original version, you would not notice what's amiss. But compare songs such as "American Pie" originally sung by Don MacLean and the new version and see the difference. Many verses have been chopped off. The new singer is singing the song and calling herself a buck (male)! Since they edited out so many verses, why did they not make the obvious changes?

Same with the movies. New releases of old classics tell one story: creative talent has run dry.

If this trend continues, we will have to learn to ride on horse and buggy all over again!

DO TRADE SANCTIONS WORK?

Not if you know how to flout the rules. For years, South Africa had sanctions placed on their goods and services, yet they survived the ordeal for years on end, while Iraq suffered the severe consequences. Both countries have what the world needed: South Africa has gold and diamonds, while Iraq has the oil. The difference is how the local businessmen circumvented the rules.

I would not have known unless someone from South Africa told me all this. This is what he had to say:

"We change the labels. Nowhere will it say "Made In South Africa". The landlocked countries around South Africa would have to export their goods via South African ports. So the labels merely state the name of one of the landlocked countries such as Lesotho. Who will know the difference?"

The candy bar cannot speak, nor can the clothes. In many cases goods are transported to a sister company in another country without the labels, and the labels attached in the host country. Those goods then get shipped all over the world. The South African businessmen continue to thrive, regardless. Now that the sanctions have been lifted on South Africa, has their economy seen any drastic improvements? Not really. Does no one stop to think why this is so?

HIDE AND SEEK

I have a very bad memory, especially when it comes to remembering where I parked my car. You can imagine, during the Christmas rush, in a huge mall parking lot, where am I going to look for the car?

For a while, I had a huge Chrysler Le Baron, and it had a luggage rack on top, so that was easy to spot. Not many cars in a parking lot have a luggage rack on their roofs. Once that car was gone from my life, I had a beat-up Hyundai, which was easy to spot because of its fading colour. Sometimes, it was difficult to remember where I parked. I used to carry a piece of paper and a pen, but that habit stopped when the pen leaked in my pocket. Then came a Nissan Micra, light blue and grey. This gave me lots of trouble in spotting it, as lots of cars were either that size, shape or colour. When my wife joined me, I had the Nissan, and she would laugh every time I forgot where I parked the car. Sometimes she would remember and steer me in the right direction. Sometimes not. The car was part of my life for three years. I had about six months to go before it was fully paid, and it was involved in an accident. The car was a write-off. With the proceeds of the insurance claim, I leased a nice Mazda Protégé. This was only 16 months old. So as soon as I saved up some money, I installed an immobilizer in the car. Now it was easy to know where I parked my car. I merely had to press the button on the remote, and follow the direction of the noise the car made when I turned on or off the alarm. The first time I did this with my wife, she was amazed that I could use such ingenuity to locate the car. Now, of course, it is second nature.

YAKITTY YAK TRAFFIC

When my wife found her first job, I used to drive her to the nearest bus stop / pick up point, where she would be picked up by the employer to drive her to the job site. I would turn on the radio to the news station to hear the traffic report, so that if the route I proposed to take had heavy traffic, I could take an alternate route. All went well, until one day she heard on the radio that the traffic was "Bumper to Bumper". She had never heard that expression before, and to her it sounded like "Bubber to Bubber". In her language, "Bubber" means "Chit Chat" or "Yakitty Yak". So, she asked me what the announcer was saying. I asked her what she meant, and in between her laughter, she managed to say: "Bubber to Bubber". I explained to her what the announcer actually DID say and what that meant, but for the next few days, she could not help but laugh every time she heard that expression.

Since her proficiency of the English language is very minimal, sometimes the words she speaks come out wrong. One of the announcer's names is Diane Newman. From my wife's mouth, this came out as "Dying Woman!" I quickly corrected her, but she persists in calling the personality by her nickname of Dying Woman. She worked with someone called "Gloria," but from her mouth it came out as "Gorilla"!

SMART CRITTERS

When I was in Mombasa, I used to rent a room at an elderly woman's house. Whenever I was at work, she would open the kitchen window to let the fresh air in. A crow would come and perch on the top of the open window. She would talk to it and sometimes even feed it. She taught the crow my name. Soon, the crow would perch on the window and call out my name. The landlady would say that I am not in, that it should return after one hour. Surely, after one hour, it would return and call out my name. How did the crow know when one hour was up? If I was home, I would answer to the crow and it would merely snicker. If I were not yet home, she would tell it to return later. How did the crow know who I was? How did it know when to return? We merely think that humans are super smart, but animals are smart cookies too. See my article on ducks crossing (Hold Mama's hands).

My brother in London had several videocassettes recorded from BBC documentary called "Daylight Robbery". This shows how clever and resourceful squirrels are. Homeowners would leave food for the birds in various containers and the squirrels would always manage to get to the food, regardless of what kinds of traps or anti-squirrel contraptions were devised to keep these creatures out.

KARMA

*I*t's true, God IS watching over us. Only He is slow to anger. Whenever we harm others, harm comes our way. I have witnessed many incidents where someone looted someone else, and thought he got away with it, only to have that person lose his house and everything else in the process. A couple of examples will make this clear.

When I was working for the insurance company in Nairobi, I heard of one agent of the company who would sell policies that generate high cash values (Endowment) to the workers in the bush. Since these peasants never had bank accounts, the agent would request proceeds payable to his agency, and in turn he would pay them cash. The folks in Head office agreed to this arrangement, and the agent would submit vouchers signed by the recipient as proof that the correct amount had been paid to the rightful customer. This went on for years. While I was in USA, this agent and his wife were flying around in a small aircraft that crashed, killing both of them. Now that the agent was no longer there to serve the customers, these customers would make their way to the Head Office whenever they needed to borrow some more against their policies. When the clerk would inform them of their current balance, the customer would be in shock! It appears that the agent only gave these peasants a modest amount of their rightful dues, and pocketed the rest. This complaint was repeated from many of the customers once served by this notorious agent. As a consequence of the agent's fraudulent activities, his two daughters, who were small children at the time of the crash, finally managed to claim against the policies on their parents' lives, after the lapse of so many years. In the mean time, inflation had made the proceeds of the policies almost worthless. These daughters were now working for someone else, for meager pay.

Another case in point: my father's sister married someone who swindled his own brother and started a biscuit (cookie) factory in Nairobi. Over the course of years, this factory did booming business, and the owner accumulated a lot of debts with his high standard of living. He had a fancy house in the posh area of town, with a hefty mortgage. A few years after I returned to Kenya, this man's business started to crumble and he had to declare bankruptcy. His children's assets were also seized to pay the creditors. Now the children, who used to drive fancy cars and live a rich lifestyle, are now reduced to working for someone else and drive around in modest, second-hand cars. Their marriages, which were not based on love for each other but rather on the family's wealth, have also dissolved.

Better to live an honest but modest life than to swindle and live a fancy lifestyle, only to have the carpet pulled from under you at a time when you least expect it.

OOBES

I was told, during my Atlanta years, that I have psychic ability and that I should hone this. I was specifically told that I could be a very good psychic healer, by laying of hands. I got to read all kinds of books on psychic phenomena, among them Out of Body Experiences (OOBES). I even joined Silva Mind Control to learn various techniques. After reading some interesting material, I decided to try out a few things. I did try my hand at OOBES, and could easily float outside my body and travel anywhere just by wishing so. I visited my younger sister whilst she was in England, and I saw her lying in bed, reading, with all kinds of stuff on her face. I called her up the next day to confirm she was actually doing this and she affirmed. I also practised by OOBES on a colleague, and the next day, she called me to say I should never do that again. She said she got the fright of her life! But she knew it was only me, and that I meant no harm.

I never did venture into psychic healing, and with today's standards, it is very risky. One can easily be accused of groping, or other inappropriate behaviour, when none is done or meant. So I have stayed away from this for now. But I do know that my hands are warmer than other people's and when I put on henna during my wedding, the colour was really dark, whereas my bride's henna colour was washed-out looking.

Even today, I can tell what someone close to me is thinking, or can pick up vibes from others. Many times, my girlfriend would call me to ask me what was the matter, and I was in my home, about 25 miles away from hers. How did she know that I was worrying over something? Similarly, I have called her up to ask, and she also wanted to know how come I know. Usually, women have the gift of gut, but when I called her up to inquire, it was an eye opener for both of us.

RACISM

*W*ho would believe that in a country like Canada, on the dawn of the twenty-first Century, racism could exist? But it does. I made a comment to my sister and brother-in-law when they came to pick me up at the airport in Toronto, in 1992, that I could feel the racism in the air. I came to discover how true this was. I could not be served in a major retail store in a prominently white neighbourhood. At first I attributed this to my accent, maybe people did not understand me, etc. But I saw more and more people in the city of all races, so surely society would be accustomed to hearing folks of all accents and dialects. I could not get a job in Toronto, so after six months I moved to Edmonton. I stayed there one year. The winters made me move again, this time to BC.

I was posted to White Rock, with the electronics retailer I worked for, and in one of the major banks, one of the tellers there was pure nasty. She would not talk that way to the white folks, but I did not know better then, or else I would have reported her to her boss. I read in the papers also how gang wars are racially motivated how innocent lives are destroyed over racist comments that lead to fights, etc.

In one newspaper, some white male had written something that said that all Government programmes exist to help the people of non-white origin, and there are no programmes in place for whites. This set my mind in motion. I replied to him stating, among other things:

That the city in which he lived, Surrey, BC was founded and developed by South Asians. This area was wilderness before, and the Punjabis (mainly) developed it. Yet the city is given a White name like Surrey. Why not an Indian name like Gangapur? The roads are named after white people (Scott Road. Who was Scott? Why not Gandhi Avenue or Nehru Highway?), the mayor of the city is white, most of his cronies are white and all the plush contracts are handed out to white companies. Where are the government programmes to address the inequity in that?

In the same edition that my reply was printed, some other people had written to counter his argument, that when immigrants come into the country, they have to start at the bottom of the ladder and move up, whereas for whites, they are handed over their futures upon a sliver platter.

The immigrants, meaning non-whites, are the ones that perform jobs that the whites are loathe to do, such as sweeping the streets, sewerage, etc., whereas the whites only wish for white collar jobs. Jobs should be handed out on merit, not skin colour. As I write this, there is a big controversy regarding nurses with foreign training, not getting jobs as nurses. The disgruntled nurses are mostly Philippinos, but the point is made. Human body is standard worldwide. The blood is the same colour, whether in Philippines or Canada, the teeth are in the same place, as the rest of the organs. So why can't a Philippino trained nurse be a nurse in any Canadian hospital? Sure, there may be some differences, such as availability of medications, but the basics don't change from country to country. Now the new Prime Minister of Canada has promised to fast-track foreign trained nurses into the Canadian health system to alleviate the chronic shortage of skilled nurses. Why did it take so long for the Government to wake up?

LEARN TO PARK

Back in my Atlanta days, one of the women I dated had a part-time job as an Avon lady, so there were always all kinds of samples laying around in the house or the car. I used to be really ticked off at people who park their cars in such a way that it takes up two parking spaces, part of one and part of the adjacent one. My dander would be up especially at times when parking was hard to find, such as Christmas season. At such times, I would leave a note for the person on his / her windshield that he / she should learn to park. On the back of the note, would be crushed lipstick, and this note would be placed under the wiper on the driver's side. Whenever the driver would see the note and remove it, the lipstick would smear all over the driver's side of the windshield. Lipstick is very hard to remove from the glass, so the message would be driven home loud and clear: LEARN TO PARK. It is highly unlikely that the driver would make commit such an offence again.

MY HONG KONG TRIP

My maternal uncle is an architect, and he landed a lucrative contract for a bank that has since collapsed. In its heyday, the bank had branches all over the world, and one of these locations was in Hong Kong. My uncle was given the contract to design various Hong Kong branches, so he was going to be stationed there for quite a while. After my trip to Switzerland, my uncle asked me to visit him, as such a chance would not recur. So after I returned to Kenya, I applied for my leave and went to Hong Kong and Bangkok via London.

My uncle had to go away on a business trip, so his wife looked after me. What I saw in Hong Kong I'll never forget. It was impressive in both good and bad ways. My uncle lived in a penthouse suite in a posh area of town. The taxi fare from the airport to his suite took less than $10 Canadian. There, the taxis are three-wheelers, and are very cheap; so much so that many people do not own cars, they merely take the taxi. My uncle never owned a car in Honk Kong.

My aunt took me to sightsee Hong Kong, and we climbed on the longest elevator in the world, on top of a mountain. It was an awesome sight.

We went shopping and I asked a pretty girl for a date, but she refused. My aunt even talked to her, but she was adamant. When my uncle returned, he explained the probable reason why she refused: she lives in a shanty and did not want a foreigner like me to know this. I saw the shanties of Hong Kong. Because of lack of space, the peasant live in make-shift boats and these boats are permanently moored in one part of the sea that has become brown with all the excreta dumped there. The peasants use the sea as their toilet. The girl I wished to date could have met me somewhere in town and I would never have to know where she lived. Oh well!

My aunt wanted to treat me to authentic Chinese food, and she insisted that I learn to eat with chopsticks, as in those restaurants, I would not be given spoons or forks. So my aunt taught me her style of holding the chopsticks, and I learnt how to use these. Of course, I could not be as fast as the natives, but for my purposes, it was adequate. Before my uncle returned, she treated me to a floating Chinese restaurant, and the food there was delicious. The boat was huge, and all the design was typical Chinese style, with the Chinese lamps, photos of pagodas, statues of Buddha, etc.

Shopping in Honk Kong is an adventure. One has to be very careful, as the same merchandise may be offered at a store nearby for less. Once a person has lived in Hong Kong for a while, he / she gets to know which stores to avoid, and to shop at those places where the locals shop. I did not have much to buy, except an AM/FM solar powered radio for a friend. I bought a couple of shirts for myself, tailor made, really cheap.

Once my uncle returned from his trip, we went to a local restaurant for Dim Sum. What a name! What about Bright Algebra? Florescent Vectors? Day-glow Calculus? Neon Trigonometry? The possibilities are endless! The experience was unique, as the place was crowded, the atmosphere thick with smoke, kids running around everywhere, and the food exquisite! We stuffed ourselves before sightseeing some more.

It is a good thing that Hong Kong was unknown to the ancient Romans, or else today, we would be calling it "Hongus Kongus"!

After Hong Kong, I visited my friend whom I met at the Swiss training center, at his native Bangkok. There he showed me some sights, we visited the famous hooker area, saw the King's Palace, and I bought a silk dressing gown for my brother's upcoming marriage. I was there only for a couple of days, so the trip was not as memorable as Hong Kong.

DEBATE

As I mentioned before, I was active in debate in High school, so it was natural for me to pursue this activity in University. The Debating society was run by the Speech Department, and it was very new, as previously, they had no staff member who could take up the challenge. We had a professor who transferred from another state (I forget which state) to Georgia, and he agreed to chair he post. When I joined the society, we had maybe three members. The topic, which was chosen nationally, was to be debated by all universities / colleges for that academic year. The topic for that year was: "Resolved, that the Federal Government should nationalize the health care system in USA." We had to do the research and be prepared to debate both points of view, i.e. Affirmative (yes, we need to change) or Negative (let the Status Quo remain). In those days, there were no such things as laptops or palmtops, so we had to carry all information on index cards. These cards would then be filed in a drawer, and be carried in special carrying cases. We also had to have cuttings (or photocopies of) the relevant articles, in case we were questioned about the legitimacy of the quote. We would be judged on various topics, e.g. Presentation, Delivery, Logic, Credibility, etc. It is one thing if our source of information was from a scientific journal or magazine, or a highly reputable newspaper (such as Wall Street Journal), and quite another matter if the source was from a gossip tabloid such as The National Enquirer. What mattered was how we presented the arguments, how we countered the other team's points, how well our points stood up to the opposing team's arguments, etc. There were two participants per team. The initial pairings would be strictly luck of the draw, and then as teams were eliminated based on the judges' impression, the contest became more fierce as we drew to the final rounds.

These debates were always held over the weekend, with most of the debates being on Saturday.

Sunday would be for the final rounds and the farewell speech, etc. Since there was only one other debate team in Atlanta, we frequently had to travel. We visited towns in Georgia such as Athens, Macon, Valdosta, and in other states as far as Mississippi or Ohio.

We would leave in the University van on Friday evenings, and would arrive at our destination motel that night. We would rest up, and meet early next morning for breakfast. From there we would make our way to the campus where the debate was being held, for registration. We would find out within the hour who we would be debating against, and at what venue. The round would last only 90 minutes, and soon after, the results would be posted, and we would then proceed to the next round. Since we were on limited budget (funded by the Department), our lunch for Saturday would be meager, but the dinner that night would be decent. We would normally go to a steak or seafood restaurant, and lunch on Sunday would once again be meager (sandwiches or so). Some towns were disasters, in that they had no decent restaurants, so we would be treated to a decent meal on the way home at any roadside restaurant.

I thoroughly enjoyed the town of Pensacola in Florida. The beach there was clean, the water warm, and we could swim in safety (no sharks). We went to certain Murfreesboro, where in the Town Square, they have a monument to the Boll Weevil (which destroys cotton plants)! In some of the towns in Alabama, we would read posters that said: "Kill a Commie for Christ," written in read to symbolize blood! Commie means communist. Some towns were so racist even then, that the blacks had their own universities, as the other universities would not accept them. Hopefully, all this has changed by now.

The debate team would grow in size, but there would always be dropouts, so there were only about five steady members at any given time. Students would drop out mainly because they could not handle rejection (if one team "slaughtered" us, the team members took the defeat personally) or because the debate interfered with their results in the other courses. We had to sign a pledge that this activity would not hamper our other studies in any way. If our grade point average fell below a certain level, we would be warned, and in subsequent quarter, be dropped from the team. That was never a problem for me. Our professor arranged so that we would be given 1 credit for the activity, and he would normally give everyone A grade.

We would be out of town two weekends out of three. The other weekend we had to update our information, learn new techniques, etc, or simply study for the coming exams.

I dropped out of the team in my senior year, but during my time, I won several trophies, including Most Improved Debater.

FRISCO, HERE I COME!

During my Atlanta days, I had a falling out with my girlfriend, so I decided we needed to cool things a bit. I had just got my brand new Mazda, and I decided to visit California during the summer holidays. Since my girlfriend lived with her mother, it was highly unlikely she would permit her daughter to cruise around with me for an extended period of time. So for those two reasons, I went sightseeing on my own. I decided to travel at night when the traffic is lighter and rest up during the day. I took the Interstate all the way. From Atlanta I went North to Tennessee, from there I cut westbound, via Missouri, Amarillo Texas, Albuquerque, the Grand Canyon, and on to San Francisco.

During my travels, I met all kinds of people. Although I would only be in any given town for a short while, some towns seemed more hospitable than others. Amarillo, Texas, for instance reeked of bigotry. I got an uneasy feeling all the time I was there and quickly made my exit. Albuquerque was a different story altogether! The people were so friendly, I seriously considered making it my home!

The Grand Canyon was a spectacular sight. I stayed there for one full night, before moving on.

On the way, I had to service my car and wash my dirty clothes. This I did in Scottsdale, Arizona, before sightseeing the Canyon. I could easily put on 750 miles a day, or rather, a night. The truck drivers were very friendly and helpful, in case there ever was a problem. USA has plenty of truck stops; these are gas stations / restaurants combined. Some of these even have mechanics on duty all times of the day. If anyone needed to fix a flat tire or do emergency work on their vehicles, these truck stops were lifesavers!

A sense of relief came over me as I crossed the border into California, though I was still far from my intended destination. I quickly made my way, and found a cheap motel to stay for the night. I must have had Someone watch over me, as the car parked next to mine was robbed during the night!

I quickly checked out of that place and looked for a place to stay for a couple of months. I found an empty attic of a nice couple's house. I did not know how to cook in those days, so I would eat out. Big deal! You could get breakfast at certain places for 99 cents that included toast, orange juice, one egg any style, grits or bacon, and all the coffee you could drink. I traveled on the cable cars a few times.

I had to see Fisherman's Wharf, and ate there a few times. That place is expensive, and on my limited budget, I had to pace myself. But the food was delicious!

I also had to see the "Crookedest Street in the World," Lombard Street. Some parts of it are more crooked than our politicians! That portion of the street is paved with cobblestones, and is very posh. The cars have to constantly steer left and right. This goes on for a few blocks only, and then straightens out. Pity our politicians never straighten out! As with any large city, the city itself is more expensive than the suburbs. So I headed out to Berkeley.

This was in the days after the Haight- Ashbury riots, so the scene was much calm and serene. At the time I passed through Haight-Ashbury, it was a slum area. Not much happening there. At UCB (Univeristy of California, Berkeley campus), there were always people on soap boxes debating this or that. But the passion and the zeal of former years had died down. No more Flower Power, LSD or Speed. I passed over the Golden Gate Bridge a few times. The toll system there was that you paid when you left San Francisco. Entry was free. I took a lot of photos of my trip, but as I mentioned elsewhere, I am jinxed. I have lost the camera and the photos.

All things must sometimes come to an end, and so did my summer holiday. I returned to Atlanta via a different route, and when I visited my girlfriend, she was relieved to see me!

ACADEMIC YEAR

*H*ave you ever wondered why the academic year begins in September? The calendar year is three quarters over by then. So what's the point? Well, to get the answers, we must look back into history.

Four to five hundred years ago, life in most of Europe was pretty much agrarian. The bulk of the population lived and worked on farms. What to do with the kids? They would come in every one's way, make pests of themselves, put their hands where they did not belong, and get sick from all the animal excrement. So in every neighbourhood, the local church would round up the kids for the day. Since they were there, they might as well learn something, so they were taught the 4 Rs, namely, Religion, Reading, (w)riting, and (a)rithmetic. This went on for nine months in the year, every year, namely from fall to spring. In the summer, the kids could stay on the farm and help with the work that needed to be done, namely gathering the crops, milking the cows, and any other chores. When harvest time came along in September or so, the kids would again get in the way, and would be sent off to the school. The cycle would begin again.

Then came the industrial revolution, and the people flocked to the cities. There, there was no such thing as an agrarian society, but the tradition prevailed. Every summer, the kids would go back to the farms and help out. Over the years, the generations lived in the cities and the farms were forgotten, but the traditions did not die. It is for this reason that the school year begins in September. In many countries where there is no winter, e.g. Kenya, the school year begins in January, and the break between classes is more evenly distributed. So instead of a three- month vacation in the summer, the kids get one month vacation at the end of

December, April, and August. This way, the parents who may also both be working, can take their vacations at other months besides the traditional months of July and August. Isn't it time we instituted such a system here in Canada / USA?

ROAD SIZE

Have you also ever wondered why the lanes of the road are only as wide as they are and no wider? If the lanes were wider, we could enjoy sitting in wider cars, and they would be more spacious, and also more comfortable. Once again, we must look to history to provide the answers.

Back in Roman times, before the advent of Jesus, the Romans built the roads in most parts of Europe. They needed roads mainly for military use. The chariots that they used could only accommodate one person standing. The road needed to be twice as wide, to accommodate one chariot going, and one coming. There were no cars, carriages, taxis, etc. in those days, so for the most part, the roads served the purpose well into the eighteenth century. Whenever societies needed extra roads, they merely duplicated the existing roads, and the lanes became as wide as they are now. With the advent of the automobile, these roads were covered in asphalt, but otherwise, they stayed the same width. So much for modern technology!

MY WIFE'S NEW PLAY TOY

When I was working at the electronics retailer in Victoria, I picked up a cordless phone that someone had given for repair, but did not bother to pick up for three months. I paid only the repair charge, of $20, and received a fully functional cordless phone. This phone served me well for a number of years. When I moved over to the Vancouver area, I used it at all my addresses except when I lived in my inlaws-to-be's basement. Since the suite was about the size of an ant's ass, there was no use for a cordless phone, so it went into storage. When my wife arrived from Fiji, she went through all my things, and asked what that item was. I explained to her, and her reaction, as usual, was: "It's garbage!" Needless to say, she made me give it away, but I warned her that in the future, should she ever decide to have one, it would have to come from her hard-earned money.

Three years later, she developed an insatiable itch for one, after seeing a cordless phone in someone's home. She has been pestering me for several months for one, and I reminded her that she would have to pay from her own resources, as she had earlier forced me to dispose of mine. We went looking for a decent one, and we saw them ranging in price from $29 and up, and the one she fell in love with was on sale at a local drugstore for $59.95. So what I paid $20 for, almost a decade ago, she paid, after tax, almost $70 for. This phone however has some features I did not have in mine, such as built-in call display that could store up to 45 numbers and an answering machine capable of storing up to 15 minutes worth of messages. So once I had the cordless phone installed, I unhooked the answering machine, which was just as well, as the AC adapter would cause a hum on the telephone line and was very annoying. I stored a few numbers in memory, and sent a warning e-mail to my friends that should they receive a phone call and my wife be on the line, it is probably because she pressed the wrong buttons! It will take her a while to get used to features of the new toy.

TIME TO GO HOME

My wife and I were on the road, hopping from one shopping mall to another. It was probably around 7:30 PM, and I was in no mood to drive to yet another mall so that my wife could search for whatever she needed. At that time, the price of gas was 85.9 cents per litre, and this was prominently displayed on the petrol station's signboard. So I pointed out to my wife that since it was almost 9:00 PM, all malls would be closing soon, so it would be best if we went home. She asked me how could it be so late so soon, and I asked her to cast her eyes straight ahead, to the gas station's sign. "See? It's almost 9:00 and the malls will close in just a minute or so." She looked and was silent for a while. It must have taken her fully ten minutes to realize that there are no clocks anywhere on the street, and what I showed her was a gas station sign, so it probably the price of gas, and not the time! I almost got away with it!

KEEP HER HAPPY

A co-worker of mine had rent out one of her bedrooms in a two- bedroom basement to a single guy, aged in his mid-twenties. Sometimes he would misbehave, and my co-worker threatened to set him up with an old lady if he did not straighten out. When she told me the tale, I asked her who she had in mind. She did not have any old ladies in mind, so I volunteered the name of our supervisor. She roared with laughter. I explained that since our supervisor was nearing menopause, what she needed was someone young to keep her happy for a while. That way she would not unburden her frustrations on her staff. While she was laughing away, she paused to consider the implications of what I had proposed. I suggested to her that she should invite our supervisor to her home on evening, have a romantic atmosphere all set up, leave the supervisor alone with the tenant, and disappear for the evening and see what would transpire! What did we have to lose but the supervisor's frustrations?

NAME THAT COUNTRY!

$\mathcal{D}$id you ever wonder how countries / cities get their names? Below is MY interpretation. You are welcome to yours!

GERMANY: Filthy Cash (Germ + money)

PAKISTAN: Father kissed Stanley (Pa Kissed Stan)

BRAZIL: Topless (Bra + zilch)

URUGUAY: You're a faggot!

PARAGUAY: A pair of faggots!

NICARAGUA: Wet panties (Knicker + agua (Spanish for water))

KENYA: Yes, I can, but can ya?

UGANDA: You're mad (You + ganda)

CHINA: No tea for me, thanks. (Chai + na)

BOLIVIA: Did you forget?

TIBET: Or not Tibet, isn't that the question?

JAPAN: Go bring me a paan (Jaa + paan)

CANADA: Incarcerate Ada (Can + Ada)

CUBA: How do you want your sugar packaged?

BARBADOS: Barbie's friend (Barbie + dos)

TURKEY: Only for turkeys like them!

ITALY: How do you like your dhosas?

LIBERIA: Where you find lots of books and magazines

MOROCCO: Proud as a peacock (More + okho)

THAILAND: Well, we can't call it Breastland or Assland!

GHANA: don't throw! (Ghaa Na cur)

SOMALIA: So Malicious!

BANGLADESH: F*** the ladies!

GREECE: What's that stuff you put on your rear end?

BAHRAIN: Give me sunshine! (Bah rain!)

DUBAI: Drowned

PALESTINE: Time to tighten your belt (Pay less time).

Ever wonder how CITIES got their names? Read below for MY interpretation:

CLACUTTA: I mowed the lawn yesterday. (Cal + cutta)

LISBON: Variation of LESBIAN

NAIROBI: Don't cry, brother. (Na ro, bhai)

LANGLEY: Crippled woman (lungree)

CLEVELAND: Well, we couldn't call it CLEAVAGE!

ABIDJAN: Go now! (Abi jaa)

POONA: don't crap here, please! (Poo + na)

BANGKOK: Go f**** a chicken! (Bang + cock)

BARCELONA: Please get it from your mother! (Baa se lo na, yaar)

PAMPLONA: The diaper's on the grass (Pampers + lawn)

ABERDEEN: Hand, is worth two….

STOCKHOLM: Stalk him

KOWLOON: Mad cow

WASHINGTON: Piles of dirty laundry (Washing + ton)

SASKATOON: Dance to mother-in-law's music (Saas ka tune)

VICTORIA: Cat scratch (Vikhoria)

ADELAIDE: Ada got laid!

BHUTAN: Ghost town (Bhoot + town)

LAHORE: The prostitute, in French. (La Whore)

MANCHESTER: Man chased her

BOMBAY: We have two kinds of bombs (Bomb + bey)

CADIZ: Eaten with khicheree

MANILLA: What kind of envelopes do you want?

BRAZAVILLE: Village where bras are made (Bras + ville)

SUVA: Candied fennel seeds

BEIRUT: What is the square root of The Bay?

After reading the names of cities, it came to me that many towns in Africa, esp. Kenya, had hidden meanings. I do not have a map of Kenya in front of me, and in the course of time, I may have forgotten many, but this is what I remember:

KIGALE: What's new? (Kee gal eh?)

KITALE: What time is it?

KAJIADO: Make a mess (kajia + do)

YALA: Oh God!

SUNA read backwards is……

KERICHO: Who's the thief? (ker eye chor?)

GILGIL: Tickle

KIJABE: Where are you going?

MACHAKOS: Fish and meat (machi + gost)

KISII: Who?

LIMURU: The ghost / spirit of Lemon (Limbu + ru)

MTITO ANDEI: Tito & I

THREE STRIKES

$\mathcal{A}$s I write this, there are three strikes going on in Vancouver area. I have very radical views on each of these, and I have made my views known, on one way or the other, to the local papers. Here they are:

STRIKE 1

The telephone workers' union decided to strike against the phone company, as they say the phone company wanted to outsource jobs to third world countries, thereby eliminating jobs in Canada. This strike dragged on for over three months. In the beginning stages, someone would physically cut the telephone cable serving various communities. At first, it was believed that the disgruntled workers were up to this, but it was later proven to be work of drug dependant vandals, who would strip off the copper to sell to support their habits. As the workers were on strike, it was the management who worked round the clock to get the wires spliced and operational again. My initial reaction was: What fools they are! Simply give the affected workers free cell phones and transfer their phone numbers to the cell phone, thereby maintaining continuity of service. Cell phone service cannot be cut by vandals. The phone company could have offered free local calling for minimum of three months or as long as the strike lasted. If the average phone bill is $30 per month, and the contract is for 36 months, that is a minimum of $1,000 per customer for cell phone revenues. If there are 1,000 customers affected, that's a cool $ million in cell phone revenues! That does not include charges for long distance calls, added services such as call forwarding, e-text, ring tones, etc. After one week, they announced that they had completed the repairs.

So what did the rival cell phone companies do? NOTHING! Why did not any rival company offer cell phone plans with free local calling for 6 months, advertise that with the strike, other service cuts could be likely, and rake in the customers? Just because one corporation is a sleeping giant, does not mean other companies should also be sleeping giants, but this is exactly what has borne out! If any cell phone provider jumped at this unique opportunity and advertised aggressively for business in BC and Alberta (provinces affected by the strike), they could easily have managed to secure $5 million in cell phone revenues! If I were a shareholder at any of these companies, I would have voted these CEOs out of office! Such opportunities do not occur frequently.

STRIKE 2

Concurrently with Strike 1, the local truck drivers went on strike, protesting high fuel prices. Consequently, goods piled up in the Port of Vancouver, as there was no one to remove the incoming goods. The railroad could only accommodate 40% of all containers, so it did not take too long for the goods to pile up. The Port eventually had to refuse any more shipment until the strike issue was resolved. While all this was happening, Wal-Mart had applied to be allowed to build a store in Vancouver. They have stores in the suburbs. Anti-American sentiment ran high in City Hall, and they refused. If I was the regional manager or CEO of Wal-Mart, this is what I would have done:

I would have bought 10 flatbed trucks, to carry containers, from any province but BC. I would have hired at least 20 truck drivers to be on company payroll, and would have sent them to BC to start releasing Wal-Mart goods from the Port. Once all Wal-Mart goods had been taken care of, any spare capacity in the trucks would then be filled with goods for other merchants. The trucks, operated by Wal-Mart Express, could be seen plying through the streets of Vancouver. After six months, I would place a nice, big ad in the local papers (or sent a missive to the Mayor) expressing the sentiment that Vancouver did not allow Wal-Mart to be located in their city, but Vancouver could not prevent Wal-Mart trucks from plying through their city. These trucks would pollute the city, use their infra structures (roads, bridges) and yet the city would not collect one dime from the company in local taxes. The end of the message would be adorned with the Wal-Mart smile, saying: "Have a Nice Day!"

Six months later, I would apply again, and see who would have the guts to refuse Wal-Mart from establishing a store in Vancouver!

STRIKE 3

After the Summer came to an end and the kids went back to school, the teachers went on strike, protesting they had not had a raise in over 3 years, classes were crowded, teacher's aides positions had been eliminated so there was no one to look after the kids with special needs, etc.

In the previous year, education was legislated to be an essential service, so it became illegal for the teachers to strike. The strike dragged on for two weeks. Meanwhile, the Courts froze the teachers' union's strike fund, forcing them to seek an early end to the dispute. Concurrently, the teachers' union was served with a class action lawsuit by the parents who had to seek baby- sitting expenses or take time off from work in lieu, to attend to their kids. I was not in favour of the strike from the very beginning, and had voiced my opinion. My suggestion:

The teachers complained that their salaries were only about 85% of the salaries for teachers in other provinces. If that was indeed true, they should have been on a go-slow mode, doing only 85% of the work. One way would be for every teacher to take two days off every three weeks, on a rotating basis by school. One day per week, every teacher should cater exclusively to students with special needs. The rest of the student could be kept busy doing homework, or else be at home. This way, the inconvenience would be minimized, and there would not be a class action lawsuit. The teachers lost two weeks of pay under the strike. If the minimum starting salary is $40,000 per year, that means, in the 2 weeks they lost at least $2,000 each ($40,000 divided by 10 months, as 2 month are summer holidays). In the go-slow mode, they would lose $400 every three weeks. The teachers can be mobilized during election time to vote against the current administration. That translates to 40,000 votes of the teachers, and if you include family, that could easily swell to well over 100,000 votes. No laughing matter!

SURROUND SOUND RAZOR BLADES

It started out as one, moved to two, became 4 and now you need a roomful to enjoy. What is it, you ask? SOUND. Our great grandfathers, if they were lucky, had a radio with ONE speaker. Along came the boomers and with them evolved the STEREO with two speakers. That served the boomers well for over 5 decades, but the manufacturers had to mess with us once more and introduced QUAD with four speakers, two in the front and two in the back. That fad died pretty soon, but not before giving birth to Surround sound with sub-woofers, and assorted speakers all over your living space.

Not to be outdone, Razor blades followed the same pattern. For thousands of years, men shaved with ONE blade system. Along came twin, and that also served the boomers well for over 5 decades. But that was not good enough so along came a THREE blade system. We have barely mastered their names and along comes FOUR blade system. Not to be outdone, its rival came out with a FIVE blade system, and both these varieties are available at a supermarket near you. Where is this going? If this trend continues, soon we will have multi-blade system with surround sound. The sound will come from you, the user, as you yell out a string of curses as you cut yourself in 53 different places with a single stroke.

But guess who else has joined this bandwagon? TOILET PAPER! In many commercial establishments such as malls and restaurant, SINGLE ply toilet paper is available, even today. In most households, they use 2 ply paper, but now one manufacturer has introduced 3 ply paper. Where will THIS go, besides down the toilet? If we have any more layers added to this tissue, every time you use it, air from between the sheets will escape, causing noise like a fart. (Remember how we as kids would blow on the side of an exercise book, and make noise? Same principle at work here). You will then exclaim: "It wasn't me!" and this time you would be right!

I SCREAM

You know the old refrain: "I scream, you scream, we all scream for Ice Cream"? Well, here are some variations on the same topic:

> (Have some Pepto Dismal ready and brace yourself)
> I paad, you paad, we all paad for IPOD
> I score, you score we all score at COSTCO
> I ching, you ching we all ching for Ka Ching (spare change)

I hop, you hop, we all hop to IHOP (Their next ad should feature a bunch of kids in a sack race all hopping to IHOP. Starring, who else but Hop-along Cassidy!)

> I sing, you sing, we all sing for Sardar Singh (RIP)
> I land, you land we all land at Ireland
> I mac, you mac, we all mac for Big Mac (Gotcha!)
> I flex, you flex, we all flex for Eye-flex (a brand of eye glasses)
> I pay, you pay, we all pay for our mistakes (Gotcha again!)
> Ye kya, woh kya, tu kya kya at IKEA
> I scold, you scold, we all scold when it's ice cold

IQ, UQ, we all Q at DQ (think of Q as a line of people; Those who are not in USA / Canada may not know that DQ = Dairy Queen = Ice Cream parlour, where there are long line-ups every summer)

> I hoe, you hoe, we all hoe at Idaho
> I hear, you hear, we're all here so let's party! (Gotcha!)

I ran, you ran, we all ran from Iran

I row, you row, we all row for Irio

I smile, you smile, we all smile for Ismail (The photographer?)

IC, UC, we all see that it's icy

I stop, you stop, we all stop for the Isotope.

I soar, you soar, we all soar above the eye sore

I laugh, you laugh, we all laugh at Olaf (The Clown?)

I wash, you wash, we all wash with eye wash (Optrex)

I browse, you browse, we all browse for eye brows